THE
ELDRIDGE
CONSPIRACY

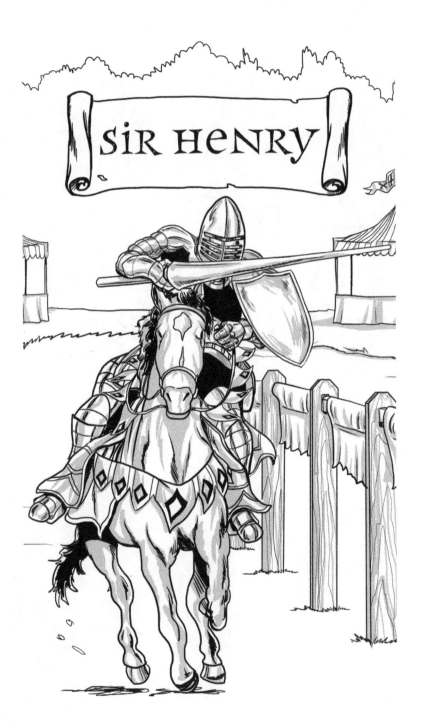

SIR KAYE THE BOY KNIGHT® BOOK FOUR

THE ELDRIDGE CONSPIRACY

Don M. Winn
Illustrated by Dave Allred

CARDBOARD BOX ADVENTURES PUBLISHING

www.donwinn.com

The Eldridge Conspiracy

ISBN: 978-1-937615-35-2 (Softcover)

ISBN: 978-1-937615-36-9 (Hardcover)

ISBN: 978-1-937615-51-2 (eBook)

Published 2017 by Cardboard Box Adventures Publishing

www.donwinn.com

The characters and events portrayed in this book are ficti-
tious. Any similarity to real persons, living or dead, is purely
coincidental and not intended by the author.

Sir Kaye, the Boy Knight® is a registered trademark of
Cardboard Box Adventures.

Printed in the United States of America.

This book is dedicated to all dyslexic and struggling readers. May you find entertainment and enjoyment as you discover characters like yourselves, and may you learn to see yourselves as people who love to read great stories.

CHAPTER ONE

I woke in the night and knew without looking that Kaye was gone. I rolled over with a groan and poked Beau where he slept curled up in a blanket nearby.

"What?" he mumbled.

"Kaye's gone," I whispered, careful not to wake the people sleeping near us in the hall.

Beau sat up, his dark hair sticking up in clumps all over his head and his blue eyes dull with sleep. He didn't look much like the queen's nephew as he scrunched up his face. "He went to find his father, didn't he?" he asked.

I nodded. "Why did he leave us behind? We're his best friends. We could help him save Sir Henry."

Beau fell backward and pulled his blanket over his face. "We don't even know what danger Sir Henry is in."

"That's what Kaye's gone to find out," I said. "Alone. He needs our help, Beau."

Moments later, wrapped in heavy cloaks, we rode our horses along the muddy road leading to the mountain pass and into the country of Eldridge. Rain pelted us with steady drops. Beau pulled his hood low over his face to keep it dry. I did the same, but my hood kept falling backwards, and the rain soon plastered my stubby, yellowish-brown hair flat to my head.

We neared the manor house where just yesterday, we had stopped a secret shipment of jewels from leaving the country after learning that the jewels were meant to pay an army to conquer our own country, Knox. Then earlier today, we had freed some prisoners from the same manor house. They had been captured and taught to cut, polish, and carve the gems.

One of those prisoners told Kaye that Sir Henry and the king of Eldridge were in danger from a powerful enemy. Right away, Kaye decided to go to Eldridge and save his father and the king.

Kaye's father, Sir Henry, was the best knight in Knox and an ambassador to the neighboring country of Eldridge. He had been living at the king's castle in Eldridge for the past two years. Kaye wanted to be exactly like him, and even though Kaye was only twelve, he had already been knighted by the queen of Knox.

Disaster struck when Kaye overestimated his strength and tried to take on two bandits at once. Another knight and a donkey saved Kaye's life. As a joke, the knight called Kaye "Sir Donkey" and the name stuck.

Then the stories began. People loved sharing ridiculous tales of Sir Donkey's stupidity, each person trying to make their story funnier than the last. Those false tales spread faster than birds could fly, until everyone thought of Sir Donkey as a joke—and the worst knight in Knox or anywhere else.

But I knew better. Kaye was my best friend, and he was a good knight, loyal and true. I yanked my hood forward to shield my face from the rain and shook my head over Kaye's unfair nickname. Within seconds, my hood slid off my head and flopped against my back again. I gave up trying to keep dry.

As Beau and I rode in front of the dark manor house, the gates creaked open. Two men leading horses stepped into the road just in front of us. A short, square man held a torch. Startled, he swung it toward our faces. We recognized each other at the same moment. They were two of the guards we had tricked when we had taken the jewels.

"Birket, look! It's Sir Donkey's ugly friend," he whispered in a raspy voice, like he had a sore throat. He looked beyond me to where Beau sat on his horse, his face shadowed by his hood. The man's lips curled into a grin. "And Sir Donkey himself on

his big, black horse! Won't the baron be pleased when we bring him the boys who stole his jewels?"

Birket, a tall, nervous man, answered, "Maybe he'll make us barons too, Fulkes, once he becomes—"

Fulkes shoved his hand over Birket's mouth. Birket clawed at it, dropping his horse's reins as he tried to free himself. "Don't go spoiling the baron's plans with your big mouth," Fulkes growled. "Grab the boys and let's go. The baron's waiting."

"Go, Reggie! Get out of here!" Beau shouted, spurring his horse forward. I snatched the torch from Fulkes and did the same. As Beau passed Birket's horse, he leaned down and scooped up the dangling reins, clucking at the confused animal. With a gentle tug, he encouraged Birket's horse to follow him, and we galloped down the road.

I flung the torch aside. It landed in a puddle with a splash and a sizzle. We pounded through the night, water flying from the horses' hooves and streaming down our cloaks. Flashes of lightning sliced through the sky, revealing towering mountaintops drawing ever closer.

Beau stopped to rest the horses for a moment at the base of the mountain path. "They'll go back for another horse," he said, "but they'll catch up soon. We have to keep going."

"What about the horse?" I asked.

"We can't just leave him out here in the rain," he said. "We'll have to bring him along. Come on, they'll be here any minute now."

Shouts in the distance proved him right. Fulkes and Birket raced along the road, getting closer with every second. Beau and I started up the mountain, our horses picking out careful steps along the slippery path. Thunder boomed, echoing among the rocks looming overhead on either side of the road. The horses walked hoof-deep through rivulets of water streaming down the stony trail. Sometimes clumps of mud and pebbles fell from above, weighted down by the rain.

I looked back down the zig-zag trail, my hood sliding off my head yet again as I did so. Silver-blue lightning showed Fulkes and Birket just two turns of the road below us. Fulkes looked up and saw me. He shook his fist and screamed at us, but the sound of the rain drowned out his words.

"Beau," I yelled. He looked back at me. "They're gaining on us. We have to go faster, or else find a way to stop them."

A splat of mud landed on my ear. I looked up and saw a heavy pile of mud teetering on the edge of the rocks overhead. Chunks of mud and rock rolled off of it from time to time, but it only needed a little push for the whole thing to fall down on our heads.

"Move!" I hollered to Beau. "Go faster!" I didn't want to be underneath that mud when it fell. We rounded a corner into another zig-zag of the road, and the path widened. No longer closed in by rock walls, we now rode along the edge of a cliff. I moved my horse Parsnip up alongside Beau and pointed to the pile of mud below us, showing him the danger we had barely avoided. Our burst of speed had left Fulkes and Birket a little farther behind. They hadn't yet reached the danger area.

During the next flash of lightning, I saw Beau jump to the ground and gather up an armful of fist-sized rocks. One after another, he hurled them into the mud pile, his aim sure and true. Bit by bit, the mud loosened and began to flow off the edge of the rock ledge. Then all at once, the entire pile fell onto the path below with a sloppy whumping noise.

Beau grinned at me and we continued climbing, hearing far-off howls of dismay from Fulkes and Birket as they turned the corner and found the path completely blocked.

"We did it!" Beau said. "That will slow them down for hours! Now we just have to get across the mountains and find Kaye."

That sounded like a good plan, but a difficult one. Eldridge was a large country, and Kaye was just a boy who had made some powerful enemies. I hoped we would find him before they did.

chapter two

Half-an-hour later, we saw tiny square lights up ahead. "It's the pass!" Beau said. The lights shone through the windows of small guard huts on either side of the road.

Because of the peace between Knox and Eldridge—peace that Sir Henry had helped bring about—the guards squinted at us, asked our business, and let us pass, advising us to get out of the rain before it got worse. Then they headed back into their little huts.

The rain fell even harder on the other side of the mountains. Beau and I rested under the shelter of an overhanging rock for a few minutes. "Eldridge is just as wet and miserable as Knox," I grumbled. "They might as well be the same country."

"They used to be the same country," Beau said.

Feeling confused, I blinked, my eyes heavy with sleep. "What are you talking about?"

"Knox and Eldridge used to be one country. A long time ago, King Aethelfred the Great had twin sons. He divided his kingdom in half before he died and gave Eldridge to the older twin and Knox to the younger."

"Beau, I'm too tired for history," I said. "I was only complaining about the weather."

I shook my shoulders, quick and hard like a wet dog, and pulled my cloak tight, flipping my soggy hood back over my head for the thousandth time.

Nothing would really dry me but a roof and a roaring fire. Hot cider sounded good, too.

Beau frowned and stared into the rainy night. "I think Kaye went to the abbey."

"What abbey?" I asked.

"One of the prisoners we freed today said that the jewels were supposed to go to an abbey on the Eldridge side of the mountain pass. He also said that a man named Azam—the same man who taught him to carve gems and told him about Kaye's father—is in charge of the gems. Azam is probably at the abbey waiting for the gems to be delivered. He doesn't know we took them yet."

"I remember he said Azam is a good man who can be trusted," I said. I also remembered that Azam had only one hand, but it seemed rude to mention it. Then I had a thought. "If Azam is in charge of the gems, he must work for the same baron that Fulkes and Birket work for. This baron wanted to use the gems to pay an army to invade Knox. How can we trust Azam if he works for the baron?"

Beau shrugged. "I don't know, but Azam can tell Kaye exactly how Sir Henry is in danger. I think Kaye will look for Azam at the abbey. We should go there too."

"What will we say when we get there?" I asked. "We can't just knock on the door and tell them we're looking for a one-handed man who's waiting for some jewels."

"Then we'll be on a pilgrimage—just two boys on a journey to see the holy sites of Eldridge. We'll knock at the abbey doors on a cold, wet night, begging admittance. The men inside are monks—religious men and scholars, book copyists and book makers. They won't refuse us shelter. In fact, they probably have holy relics inside the abbey we can look at. They'll be more than happy to show us. They probably have many visitors who come to see their sacred treasures."

I frowned in the dark. "Their holy treasure is probably a pig bone they say is the sacred knucklebone of St. Ethelberg the Misfit."

"You're awfully pessimistic, Reggie," Beau said.

"You would be too if all your life your father had threatened to send you to school with the monks because you were too stupid to know your right hand from your left."

"You're not stupid," Beau said. "You just get lost easily. Let's get going. I want to get off this mountain."

My gloom lifted for a moment and I poked Beau in the arm. "Hee-hee, Fulkes thought you were Sir Donkey."

"And I was insulted! I'm three years older than you both and a whole head taller. How dare he mistake me for someone so short!"

I followed Beau down the mountain, yawning until I thought my head would split. I hadn't slept much that night, and riding a horse was never relaxing for me. Especially not after midnight on the side of a muddy mountain with patches of loose stones making the horse's feet slide.

Eventually we returned to flatter ground, where we found a small, dark village huddled at the mountain's feet. "We should have asked the guards at the pass about the abbey," Beau said. "It's far too late to knock on someone's door to ask for directions now."

"There's only one road," I said. "We might as well follow it."

"We need to rest the poor horses," Beau said. "They've been working so hard. What's this?" By a flash of lightning, we noticed an old burned-out house with half a roof at the edge of the village.

"Half a roof is better than none," Beau said. "Come on." We managed to fit all the horses inside and then curled up near them under our wet cloaks. "If we had dry wood, we could build a fire," Beau said.

"We don't have dry anything," I said, "Nothing in this entire country is dry."

"The abbey should be dry," Beau said. "Think about it, hot fires, hot food, and a bed that's not next to a wet horse. We'll have all that soon."

I shivered under my clammy cloak. "Beau, why did Kaye leave us behind?"

I heard a flapping noise that must have been Beau's wet cloak moving as he shrugged. "He probably thought we'd stop him."

"I would have gone with him," I said.

After another flapping noise, Beau said, "Maybe he wants to save his father by himself. He's certainly wanted to do things alone before."

"But this is a big thing," I said. "He'll need help."

"He'll have it. We'll find him, don't worry."

"Maybe he's still upset that everyone calls him Sir Donkey now," I said. "Maybe he thinks he can end it by saving his father and the king from whatever danger they're in."

"Maybe," Beau said with a yawn. "Saving the king would make Sir Donkey famous for doing something good for a change. Don't worry, Reggie. We'll find him. Go to sleep."

I couldn't help worrying as I lay there. I worried that Kaye might do something dangerous and heroic just to prove to the world that he was no Sir Donkey. I wished I could help him lose that name. I wished he had taken me with him when he left.

I crinkled my nose. Everything—even my skin—smelled like wet horse. I took turns worrying about Kaye and sniffing my arm in disbelief until I finally fell asleep.

CHAPTER THREE

Beau woke me in the gray light before dawn. "It stopped raining," he said. "Let's go."

My stomach felt so empty, it tied itself into knots, but I kept quiet and saddled my horse. I was tired of hearing myself complain, and I'm sure Beau was too.

As we rode, the birds sang themselves into fits of joy over the coming day. The sky grew pink and golden, and the birds fell silent as the tiniest sliver of sun like molten steel peeked over the edge of the world. Then it popped up into the sky all at once, the birds so wild with excitement that you'd never think it happened every day.

Beau whistled a cheery tune and I rode up alongside him. "I'm sorry I was grouchy yesterday," I said. "I was wet and worried about Kaye."

"You're still wet and still worried," Beau said. "What's different now?"

"The sun's up, I guess. I can see where I'm going. And you promised a fire and maybe a bed later at the abbey."

He nodded. "And soup. At least, I hope they have soup. There's a cold spot inside me that only hot soup will fix."

"I was thinking about hot cider last night," I said with a laugh. "It's almost fall. Look at the trees." Tiny patches of orange and yellow edged a few clumps of leaves in the trees along the road.

Soon we came to a crossroads in a village with an old gray church. People moved about, stopping to eyeball the strangers riding through.

"Pardon me," Beau asked a man nearby. "We're looking for the abbey. Can you tell us how to get there?"

The man grunted. "Most boys would be helping with the harvest these days, not traveling about to abbeys. We barely got the wheat and barley under cover yesterday before the rain came to spoil it." He yawned. "And now there's threshing to do." He yawned again. "Wislett Abbey is the closest. Keep following this road and you'll find it."

"Thank you," Beau said. "Good day to you, sir."

As we passed the old church, I heard a familiar neigh. "Wait. That sounds like Kadar," I said. Sure enough, Parsnip whinnied back, as if greeting an old friend.

We rode behind the ancient building and found Kaye's fine warhorse Kadar grazing under an apple tree at the edge of the churchyard. He nickered to our horses like they had been parted for months and sniffed at Acorn, which is what I had named Birket's roly-poly brown horse. Then Kadar went back to munching the apples littering the ground.

Kaye sat under the same tree. He held a parchment in one hand and a half-eaten apple in the other. "What took you so long?" he asked. "I've been waiting for you."

I scowled at Kaye. "Why didn't you just take us with you in the first place?"

"Because you would have tried to stop me," he said. "And just so you know, I'm not going back. I'm going to find my father and warn him that he and the king are in danger."

"We know," Beau said, sliding off his horse.

I stared at Kaye's hand. "Are you eating apples from the churchyard?"

He took a bite. "Why not?"

I swept my hand around the yard, which seemed empty except for a few flat stones. "There are people *buried* here!"

"It's public land, and anyway, they're not eating them," Kaye said. "These are good apples. They shouldn't go to waste."

I shook my head at Kaye.

He shook his back at me. "Look, I found something important. This was nailed to the church door."

"You took it off the church door?" I said. "That's worse than eating apples from the churchyard!"

"Well, I'm not putting it back. You'll see why. Listen." He read aloud from the parchment, *"Know ye here men of Eldridge, ye have been wickedly deceived by one who claims the throne. King Aldric of Eldridge is not of noble blood, but is a changeling.*

"Ye must know that his adoptive mother the Queen was delivered stillborn of a daughter, but so as not to disappoint her King and Nation of an heir, she sent to find another newborn babe to take the dead infant's place. It was a butcher's son she took for her own, and this is he whom you now call King Aldric. This secret did the queen confess on her deathbed to Edward, Eighth Bishop of Hemrick.

"Know ye that the real ruler of Eldridge by right of being a true-born offspring of the glorious King Aethelfred is Baron Thomas of Denbrooke, who seeks to set right this terrible wrong as glory demands his station in this world.

"Know ye also, that the celebrated Sir Henry of Knox is naught but a liar, a traitor, and an enemy to Eldridge. He speaks sweet words of friendship and peace, but his heart is black with hatred for Eldridge, and he is determined to destroy it and bring war to our fair land. Only Baron

Thomas will expose him for what he truly is when the time is right. Put no faith in so-called kings who treat with the enemy."

Kaye's hands shook. "How dare he say this about my father! This is ridiculous!"

"What does that even mean?" I asked.

Beau frowned and explained. "It says King Aldric is an imposter, substituted as a baby for the queen's child who died. Then it says that Baron Thomas is the one with royal blood, the one who should really have the throne. It sounds like he's planning to take it."

"Maybe that's why the king's life and Sir Henry's life are in danger," I said. "Baron Thomas seems to hate them both. Maybe he's their enemy."

"He's their enemy and a liar!" Kaye sputtered. "My father's no traitor to Eldridge or Knox. He left us to come here to *keep* the peace. It was a noble thing for him to do." Kaye stared at the words on the parchment. "My father cares about Eldridge and about peace. He made a great sacrifice to come here. That's what I've been told every day since my father left us. There's no way he came here to destroy Eldridge."

Kaye crushed the parchment into a loose ball between his hands. "We're going to the abbey," Kaye said. "We'll look for that man Azam. If he said my father and the king are in danger, he must know more about Baron Thomas' plans. When we find him, he'll tell us more about this conspiracy and then we can decide what to do."

Beau smirked at me. "I *told* you he'd start by going to the abbey to find Azam."

"Then let's go," Kaye said. "We can be there this afternoon if we start now."

"Do you have any food?" I asked. "We haven't eaten for hours. I didn't bring any with me."

"You could eat an apple," Beau said. I glared at him.

"You forgot to bring food?" Kaye asked, lifting his eyebrows toward the sky.

I blushed. "Well, you were gone," I said to Kaye. "And it was dark and I was worried."

Kaye chuckled. "Amazing," he said. "If you were so worried about me that you forgot to bring food—that's really touching." He shoved my shoulder. "And fortunately for you, I did bring food."

He handed us some bread and dried meat. It wasn't much, but the meat was so tough that chewing on it felt like eating a much bigger meal than swallowing it did. I chewed thoughtfully as we rode along.

I thought about how the queen of Knox once offered to knight me, but I chose to become a Royal Chronicler instead. My job was to write down all the adventures that Kaye and Beau and I had together. We had already had a lot of adventures, but I hadn't written about any of them yet. I had terrible handwriting that no one could read and it took me so long to write anything that I was afraid to start.

"I figured something out," I said, once I had swallowed the last of the meat.

"What?" Kaye asked.

"I was worried I made a terrible mistake choosing to be a Royal Chronicler instead of a knight because I thought I had to be one or the other." I looked at Kaye and frowned, "That's your fault."

He crossed his arms and said, "What are you talking about?"

"Well, nothing matters more to you than being a knight. You've never wanted to be anything else. So I thought I had to choose just one thing to do too. But the truth is, I can do a lot of things."

"Like what?" Beau asked.

"Well, sometimes I can be a Royal Chronicler, and other days I can be more like a knight. I can be a jouster or a jester or… or…a roof-thatcher! It doesn't matter! I can be anything I want. I don't have to choose just one thing for the rest of my life."

"Do you know how to thatch roofs?" Kaye asked.

"No," I said, hesitating for a moment.

"You might want to learn," Beau said with a laugh. "What if you fell through the roof and into the house? You'd land in the porridge pot."

"Don't make fun of me," I said. "Just think about it. We can be anything. Today we're adventurers and spies in a strange country."

Kaye and Beau both grinned. "I like the sound of that!" Kaye said.

"Me too," Beau said. "Let's get on with our adventuring!"

Afternoon shadows slanted long across our path before we arrived at the open gates of Wislett Abbey. We rode inside the protective walls of the abbey and saw a large stone building. The building looked old, like it had grown out of the stony ground long before Eldridge or Knox existed. Several monks worked busily in the abbey gardens, grubbing with hoes and spades in the vegetable patch. My stomach growled as I thought of a hot dinner. Even vegetables sounded delicious.

As we dismounted, a long-legged monk strode toward us, his black robes flapping in the breeze. Under his cowl, his deeply-lined face looked serious, but the smile in his tired blue eyes made us feel welcome. He carried a pot of honey.

"Greetings, my sons. I am Brother Antony. What brings you to our humble abbey today?" he asked in a deep voice.

"We are on a pilgrimage, Brother Antony," Beau said. "We heard you had many holy relics here."

"Yes, of course," Brother Antony replied. "We are the guardians of several holy relics, as well as some famous historical items, like the sword of King Aethelfred the Great. It is a little-known fact that he spent his last days here at this abbey as he fled for his life."

"Why was he in danger?" I asked.

Brother Antony chuckled. "That is a tale best saved for *after* eating, I believe. Please, join us for our evening meal and stay the night here. We have shelter and food for your horses." He sniffed in our direction. "And good strong fires to dry your clothes. Come, follow me."

He gestured to another monk, who led our horses to the stable while we followed Brother Antony into the dim silence of the abbey.

chapter four

Brother Antony led us into the abbey and then out again into a courtyard, passing a large room to the right.

"This is our library," he said. "It's famous in Eldridge. Many of the brothers here are fine copyists and artists as well."

A wide, green courtyard shaded by four giant oak trees lay at the center of the abbey. Acorns dropped onto the soft grass with tiny thumping noises as a breeze stirred the oak leaves.

"Those trees are *huge*," I said in wonder.

Brother Antony nodded. "Legend says they were planted the day the abbey was finally completed. As you can see, those trees have been growing for hundreds of years."

We walked along the abbey's cloisters—long, shady, arched halls supported by columns of stone. One side of the cloisters opened out to the central green area. The solid inner wall of the cloisters had many doors set into it that probably led back inside the abbey building.

Several monks strolled through the cloisters, enjoying the soft wind, and no doubt thinking of scholarly things. One monk sprawled in the grass inside a splash of light, soaking up the last warm rays of the sun before it dipped below the abbey walls.

Brother Antony pointed to a small tower in the corner of the courtyard. "That, my sons, is the room where King Aethelfred the Great drew his last breath, safe within the shelter of the abbey walls."

"Can we see it?" Kaye asked.

"Perhaps," Brother Antony said, sounding doubtful. "An important guest is staying in the tower right now. He admires King Aethelfred greatly and often comes to meditate on the life of the ancient king. We cannot disturb him. But after he leaves, you are welcome to see King Aethelfred's room."

Brother Antony led us to the abbey's great hall. Dozens of tables covered with smudged gray cloths filled the room and a bright fire crackled in a large fireplace.

"Spread your clothes over some benches in front of the fire," Brother Antony said. "If you turn them a few times, they should dry. Warm yourselves as well. The nights are growing colder." He chuckled. "When the leaves and my nose begin to turn red, it's a sure sign that winter isn't too far away."

He carried his pot of honey away, and we dragged benches in front of the fire. Kaye spread his cloak over one bench and draped his stockings, tunic, and leggings over another. He propped his boots in front of the fire and stood there in his linen underclothes.

"Kaye!" I gasped. "What are you doing?"

"Drying off," he said. He stretched his arms out and turned around and around so all of him could dry. "I don't like being damp. It makes me itchy. I wish I could have a bath, too."

Beau laughed and took off his clothes as well. "I don't think these monks bathe very often. Their black robes hide a lot of dirt, and most of them look rather...dusty."

"Come on, Reggie, dry off," Kaye said. "Nobody cares. The monks have their minds on more important things than clothes."

"Or lack of clothes," Beau said.

I soon stood in my underclothes too. None of the monks passing through the room paid any attention to us. It felt good to be warm, light, and free after spending most of last night feeling cold, damp, and almost smothered under my heavy, wet cloak.

My nose began detecting some appetizing smells. "I think the food is here," I said. Sure enough, several monks entered the room carrying platters of food. I didn't know what kind of food monks ate, but I hoped there would be plenty of it.

I wasn't disappointed. I had heard of monks who ate only dry crusts of bread, but not these monks. Their food was plain, but good, and they ate it in silence, enjoying every bite.

We ate a heaping dish of potage—a pale, ugly-colored porridge made of peas and oats. It tasted bland, but it filled our empty stomachs with hot, satisfying food, warming us from the inside out.

For the rest of the meal, we ate dark bread and hard cheese, along with fresh plums and oatcakes. The nutty, buttery oatcakes crumbled in my mouth, crunchy and faintly sweet with honey from Brother Antony's bees.

I finished the meal with fruit, slurping down sweet plum juices as I kicked my feet under the monks' dirty tablecloth.

I reached for another plum and accidentally knocked it underneath the table.

"I'll get it," Beau whispered, ducking below the tablecloth.

A moment later, Kaye's green eyes sharpened as he looked over my shoulder.

"What's wrong?" I whispered, twisting to look behind me. Beau crawled out from under the table and handed me my plum. He looked behind me too, but we didn't see anything.

"Two men just walked through here," Kaye said. "I remember them from the manor house. The short one laughed when I cut my hand before we escaped."

He held up his left hand, tightly wrapped in a ragged bandage covering his palm.

"Fulkes and Birket," I whispered. "They work for the baron. We met them on the road last night. They tried to capture us."

Beau snorted with laughter. "We dumped a pile of mud in their path and trapped them so they couldn't follow us."

"But why did they come here to the abbey?" Kaye hissed at us.

"They were supposed to deliver the jewels here," I said. "Maybe they came instead to deliver the news that the jewels are gone."

"Do you think they saw us?" Kaye asked.

I looked around the hall. In a sea of dirty gray tablecloths and black-robed monks, our white underclothes stood out like a bonfire on a dark night.

"Oh, I think they saw us," I said.

We ate the rest of our meal in silence, keeping wary eyes on the various doors of the hall, but we saw no more of the baron's men.

CHapteR five

After eating, we dressed in our now-dry clothes, and Brother Antony rejoined us, along with a little round monk named Brother Francis. "Forgive me for not sitting with you at dinner, but as you can see, we don't speak during meals, preferring to spend them in silent contemplation of holy things," Brother Antony explained.

I frowned. Most of the monks at our table had seemed to be contemplating their food. I had almost felt a connection with them. I liked their peaceful abbey with its giant trees, long history, and shaded cloisters. I enjoyed their simple, good food.

Brother Antony showed us King Aethelfred's portrait hanging over the fire. King Aethelfred's dark eyes shone with kindness and wisdom, but his long, droopy hair and long, droopy moustache made him look sad. Tall and thin, he wore a suit of armor and a long red cloak. He carried a small, plain shield and a large, plain sword. Three small pinkish-red balas rubies adorned the thin gold crown on his head.

"I'll tell you about King Aethelfred's death, as I promised." Brother Antony sat on the floor and leaned against one of the benches, his long robe puddling around him, almost, but not quite covering his bony ankles.

When I looked closer, I could see sticky streaks on his robe that must have been honey, but those streaks were now coated with dust and lint.

Brother Antony cleared his throat. "Hundreds of years ago, King Aethelfred ruled over both Eldridge and Knox. It was one kingdom at the time, and King Aethelfred ruled over it wisely and well. However, his oldest sons—a pair of twins—were not like him at all. They were both foolish and thoughtless men."

"So what happened?" Kaye asked.

Brother Antony sighed. "In his wisdom, King Aethelfred thought it was unjust to give the kingdom to one son instead of the other—after all, they were twins, and each one was one half of the other. So, near the end of his life, he divided his kingdom, leaving half of Eldridge to the older twin, and giving the other half, the new country of Knox, to the younger twin."

"That seems fair," I said.

"The older twin was secretly furious. How dare the king take away half of his kingdom! He had grown up expecting to rule the entire kingdom by himself one day—always ending every argument with his twin with the words, 'Well, someday I shall be king, so there!'"

Brother Francis leaned forward and grinned, "This was not dignified behavior in a grown man who already had three children of his own."

We laughed, and Brother Antony continued his tale. "The older twin's dark feelings simmered below the surface, like a pot of soup on the fire under a tight lid. Finally one evening, he lured his twin up to the old castle's highest tower—and it was a *very* high tower, because the old castle was built on the edge of the mountain."

Brother Francis explained, "The new castle is built at the bottom of the mountain, close to the city of Rombauer. The old castle lies in ruins high above it, like a dark cloud."

Brother Antony continued his tale. "As they gazed at the stars and spoke of the future, the younger twin never suspected the grief and rage in his brother's heart until the moment the older twin pushed him over the edge of the tower. At the last second, the older twin remembered how he loved his brother and all the years they had spent together. He reached out to save him, grabbing hold of his hand, but it was too late."

"Did he die?" I asked.

Brother Francis nodded. "They both fell, landing together at the bottom of the mountain."

Brother Antony cleared his throat a bit. "They were born together, and they died together. It was not meant that one should be on this earth without the other, although they didn't know it until it was too late. And poor King Aethelfred's heart broke at the same time his sons' bodies broke."

"To make things worse," Brother Francis added, "many of the nobles felt that the kingdom should not have been divided. They rebelled, and war filled every city and village of Eldridge."

Brother Antony's solemn voice finished the story. "Like the tide of a great sea, the war rose to the king's own castle, high on the mountain. Servants within the castle betrayed their king and he nearly died. Full of grief and despair, he fled, finding refuge here in the walls of this sacred abbey. He called for the Bishop of Newksbury, and the bishop came. The king and the bishop met together for several hours, and the bishop left soon afterward carrying an important-looking document."

"What was the document?" Beau asked.

With a shrug, Brother Antony replied, "We do not know. The bishop, traveling alone, fell into a well and drowned just after leaving here. The monks discovered the bishop's body only when his horse returned to the abbey with an empty saddle. The document must have been lost or ruined. Otherwise it would be in the library here at the abbey. The monks never told the king of the bishop's death, but sheltered him for the few hours he had left to live. I hope and pray that he found peace as he rested, because he died of sorrow shortly afterward."

"So how did they solve the problem of the divided kingdom?" Kaye asked. "Knox still exists, so the king must have had his way in the end."

Brother Francis explained. "The wives of the twins pleaded with the nobles to let the past go and to let their infant kings— the oldest sons of the twin princes—grow in peace to become the kind of rulers the people deserved. The nobles heard their pleas and over time, they accepted the two kingdoms."

"And now," Brother Antony added, "very few people remember or care that Knox and Eldridge were once one country. But here in Eldridge, feeling sorry too late, we still remember King Aethelfred each year on the day of his death. We call it King Aethelfred's Day of Remembrance, and it approaches in three days' time."

"What a sad story," I said.

Brother Antony smiled. "Not all stories about King Aethelfred are sad," he said. "There's one I call King Aethelfred and the Insulting Jester. It's my favorite."

"What happened?" I asked.

"A traveling fool, or jester, once entertained King Aethelfred in his throne room. The people were ready for some fun, but the fool was disappointing. He made no one laugh with his jests, and finally, full of anger, he insulted the king to his face. Enraged, the king stood up, threatening to lock him in the tower for his insolent behavior. The man laughed, and said that he had heard so much about King Aethelfred's wisdom, yet when insulted, the king behaved just like any common man, no better or worse than the jester himself."

"Did he lock the jester in the tower?" Beau asked.

Brother Antony shook his head. "The king admitted it was true, he was no better than the jester, but he also said that unlike the jester, he at least had the power to make people laugh. He lifted his arms in the air and dropped them down suddenly and sharply. As he did so, he opened the very ground beneath the insulting jester and the man disappeared! The court roared with laughter at the sight of the man's face as he fell through the floor and into the earth below."

"Was the king so powerful he could command the very earth to open?" I asked in amazement.

Brother Francis laughed. "No, my boy. There was a trapdoor in the floor. The next day, when they pulled the jester out, he was a humbled man."

I opened my mouth to ask another question, but it turned into a yawn so big I heard my jaw crack.

Brother Antony smiled. "You are tired from your journey. I will take you to your room and tomorrow I shall show you the abbey. You can see our holy relics, and the library and the scriptorium where some of our brothers make books. If time permits, I will even show you my bees," Brother Antony said.

"Thank you, Brother Antony," Beau said. "We are grateful for your hospitality."

We said good night to Brother Francis, and Brother Antony led us down a narrow hall to a tiny room where three pallet beds filled the entire floor.

"Please stay in your room this evening," Brother Antony said. "The brothers often walk about in silent contemplation, and you could disturb their meditations if you were to leave your cell. Good night, my sons. Sleep well."

"Good night, Brother Antony," we replied as he left us.

Beau flopped down on a bed and sighed. "It feels so good to stretch out," he said.

"Don't get too comfortable," Kaye said. "I think we should do some exploring."

"But Brother Antony said we had to stay in our room," I said.

"Nonsense," Kaye said. "We'll wear our dark cloaks and stay in the shadows. We won't disturb anyone. I want to see that room King Aethelfred died in."

"I didn't know you were so interested in history," Beau said.

"I'm more interested in the important guest who's staying there right now," Kaye said. "Maybe it's Azam."

"And maybe it's not!" Beau said. "It could be a bishop or a visiting priest. For all you know, the king of Eldridge himself is staying there tonight."

Kaye scowled at Beau. "Well, if it *is* the king, then we can warn him that his life is in danger."

"Let's do it," I said, feeling excited enough that I forgot how sleepy I was. I loved exploring.

"It's not a good idea," Beau said. "We're guests here. We should respect the rules."

"Oh, hush, Beau," Kaye said. "We're just taking a little walk. You can stay here if you want to."

"Oh, no," Beau said. "You're not leaving me out of the adventure again. I hated hiding in the forest so no one would recognize me the whole time you were at the manor house. Let's go."

We slipped out of our room and Beau reluctantly followed.

"Watch out for Fulkes and Birket," I whispered. "We know they're here."

Tiptoeing along, we stuck to the shadows in the cloisters until we stood across from the tower room. We saw a light and heard voices inside. Angry voices.

chapter six

Close-growing vines twined around the walls of the tower room. We crouched below a narrow arched window glowing with firelight inside its leafy frame.

"What do you mean a *child* took the jewels?" a deep voice roared with fury.

"We thought it was a monster, Baron Thomas," Birket said in his always-frightened-sounding voice.

"It *was* a monster," Fulkes said gruffly. "It came roaring out of the woods, making the most horrible sounds and waving its arms, looking like nothing we'd ever seen."

We grinned at each other. That was *our* monster they were talking about.

"We ran for our lives," Birket said.

Fulkes added, "It was all a trick though. The boy did it to scare us off while he took the jewels. It was the child knight of Knox—the little pet of the queen."

The baron screamed, "That's ridiculous! How dare he!" He stopped short. "Wait…the child knight of Knox—do you mean to say that *Sir Donkey* took my jewels so now I can't pay my army? What an insult! He's a joke—nothing more than a jester to the whole country of Knox. If that boy's a knight, then I'm a boot."

"My lord, you're no boot!" Birket cried out.

"And Sir Donkey is no knight!" the baron yelled.

"Oh, no," Kaye whispered. "I can't believe that stupid nickname has even spread to Eldridge. I'll never live this down." He sighed. "I suppose even my father has heard it by now."

Almost as if he had heard Kaye's words and followed his thoughts, the baron said, "Sir Donkey is young Balfour, son of Sir Henry, isn't he?"

"My lord," Birket began, but Fulkes interrupted.

"Yes, Baron Thomas," he said, his raspy voice grating on my ears. "His name is Kaye Balfour. That's why some call him Sir Don-Kaye."

"That's preposterous!" Baron Thomas said with a huff. A shadow paced back and forth across the room. "I hate that rotten little knight *and* his stuck-up father. They call Sir Henry the best knight since King Aethelfred himself. How dare they compare him to King Aethelfred? I'll fix him! I'll show everyone how terrible Sir Henry *really* is. *I* am most like King Aethelfred! *I* am his true heir!"

"Of course, my lord," Fulkes said.

"And King Aldric the imposter just loves him," the baron continued. His voice took on a mocking tone as he mimicked the king, "I don't know where we'd be without Sir Henry. He alone has helped us create and keep the peace between Knox and Eldridge."

"My lord," Birket whispered.

"Silence! I have a better idea for keeping peace. I'll take the throne that is rightfully mine and unite both countries, the way it *used* to be under the rule of my noble forefather King Aethelfred the Great. I shall be just like him, and Eldridge will once again enter a golden age."

"How will you do that?" asked Fulkes.

"With your help," the baron said. "Ride to Kingsbridge tomorrow and find Azam. He's at the Pigpenny Inn in Cotswold Lane. Tell him the jewels are gone and we must go with my other plan. He'll give you more instructions and supplies from my warehouse. And if he doesn't, I have ways of making him. Remind him of that." He chuckled.

"Yes, my lord," Fulkes and Birket said together.

"Then get yourselves to Rombauer Castle early on the Day of Remembrance and set up everything exactly the way Azam tells you to. We only have one chance to do this, so it has to be just right."

"Yes, my lord," they said.

"And before you leave tomorrow, go to the scriptorium under the library and get a bag of the placards the monks made for my cause. We've put placards up all over Eldridge already—everywhere except Rombauer City, the king's own city. That's your job. Put them up on every wall in Rombauer City."

"Yes, my lord," Fulkes said.

"And do it before King Aethelfred's Day of Remembrance! That's when I'll take the throne. I have the support of many nobles—they're angry at the way King Aldric has wasted so many chances to make this country rich and prosperous. But the rest of the nobles need to be ready to accept me as king once that imposter Aldric is out of the way. The placards will help with that. As for Sir Henry, I'll soon be rid of him forever, and I'll never have to hear anyone compare him to King Aethelfred ever again!"

"My lord," Birket began for a third time.

"What is it, Birket?" he shouted. "What's wrong with you? Why do you keep whispering at me?"

"That boy. Sir Donkey. He's *here*," Birket answered in his breathless voice.

"That's ridiculous! What are you talking about? How could he be here? Why is he here?" Questions popped out of the baron's mouth faster than bubbles rising to the surface of a pond.

"I saw him." Birket's voice trembled as he added, "*And* his ugly little friend. They were at dinner with the monks, sitting in their underclothes, eating oatcakes and plums, as happy as you please."

"Ridiculous," Baron Thomas muttered. "Are they still here?"

"I don't know," Birket said.

"Well *you're* useless, aren't you?" Baron Thomas sneered. "Get out of my sight! Go to bed. I'll see the abbot about this Sir Donkey business. If that boy is really here, I'll make him suffer for stealing my gems."

"Yes, Baron Thomas," the men murmured. We darted into the shadows as they came out the door. Fulkes walked like a bulldog, short and square and powerfully built, with a stubbly beard and an angry expression on his face like he had just stubbed his toe. Birket looked slim and anxious, with bony wrists and an unusually large Adam's apple bulging out of the middle of his long neck.

We watched them until they left the cloisters. Then Kaye whispered, "What is he planning to do to my father?"

"I think he's going to kill him *and* the king," Beau said.

"He'll do it on King Aethelfred's Day of Remembrance," I added.

"That's in three days," Kaye said. "We have to find out Baron Thomas' whole plan before then, or my father will die."

"He really hates your father," I said.

"He hates me too," Kaye said cheerfully.

"Why are you happy about that?" I asked.

"If he hates me, it means I'm more like my father than I thought. After that Sir Donkey business, I didn't think anyone would ever take me seriously as a knight again."

"Um, Kaye," Beau said, "he doesn't. He called you ridiculous."

"I know," Kaye said, "but if he hates me, it means I matter to him. I ruined some of his plans already, and if I can find out about the rest of his plans, I'll ruin them too. I'll ruin everything I can. And when he fails, he'll know it's because of me. *Then* we'll see how much he hates me."

I frowned. This didn't sound like the Kaye I knew, but I decided not to say anything. We peeped in the tower window. Baron Thomas sat on the floor before a fire, his back to us. He held an ancient-looking sword in both hands, moving it so that the firelight rippled up and down the blade. After a while, he bent his head and rested it on the flat of the blade.

"I shall try to be worthy," he muttered in his gruff voice.

chapter seven

We backed away from the tower room. "If Baron Thomas finds us here, we'll never reach my father in time," Kaye said. "We need to leave, but I want to see this scriptorium first."

"What's that?" I asked.

"It's where the monks copy their manuscripts," Beau whispered as we scuttled along the cloisters like frightened beetles, clinging close to the shadowy walls of the abbey.

"Shh," Kaye said as he eased open the big abbey doors. He waved us into the library and headed for a single torch that burned near a door on the far side of the room.

"I want to see what's in here," Kaye said, lifting the torch off the wall and opening the door. We found a deserted room, full of slanted tables and pots of dark ink. One table held supplies for mixing colored paint. A single page of a manuscript sat on that table, showing a tiny, colorful picture of a king speaking to a crowd of people inside a giant letter O. Flowers and leaves adorned the margins of the page, picked out with spots of bright gold paint, but Kaye didn't leave us any time to admire its beauty.

"Come on, there's another door here," he said. The door opened onto a staircase leading downward. Another door at the bottom stood partly open. Kaye peeked into the crack, and seeing no one, he pushed it open wider.

"Aha!" he said triumphantly. "Look—it's a workshop for writing those placards. There are hundreds of them."

He was right. Piles of parchments identical to the one Kaye had taken from the church door waited for Baron Thomas' men to take them away and spread their traitorous message.

Kaye shoved the torch into my hand, found a large cloth bag, and began stuffing placards into it. "There are more bags over there. Fill them up too," he said.

"What are you doing?" Beau asked.

"These placards are part of Baron Thomas' plan to become king of Eldridge and hurt my father," Kaye said. "I told you, I'm going to find out his plans and ruin everything I possibly can. Right now I'm ruining *this* part of his plan. If we take these away, Baron Thomas can't have his men put them up in Rombauer City."

"He'll just make more," I said. "And they're already posted all over the rest of Eldridge. It's too late."

"No, it's *not*," Kaye said fiercely, shoving parchments into the bag. "He wants to put these placards up for the people of Rombauer City to see before the Day of Remembrance. I can't stop him from putting *any* placards up, but I can stop him from putting up *these* placards."

Beau looked at me and shrugged. He picked up another bag and began pushing placards into it willy-nilly. I grabbed another empty bag, but couldn't do anything with it since I held the torch, so I kept arguing with Kaye. "Kaye, it would be better to just go and find Azam and learn what he knows. This is a waste of time. Someone is sure to catch us."

"I'm not leaving without these placards," Kaye said. "After we find out the baron's plan, we'll go tell the king and my father, and we'll need the placards to show them just how dangerous Baron Thomas is."

Beau made a face and said, "I think they'll realize that when we tell them Baron Thomas plans to kill them."

Kaye frowned. "No, it's not enough. We have to show him everything we've been through to help him. Then he'll understand."

"Understand what?" I asked.

Kaye didn't answer. He was too busy grabbing armfuls of placards to bother with me anymore. He worked his way to the front of the room, where he snatched placards off a table in the dark until I felt bad and carried the light closer to him.

"Kaye, watch what you're grabbing. Some of those parchments looked different. I think you took something else."

"I don't care," Kaye said. "If it's in this room, it has something to do with Baron Thomas' plan, and we're taking it. We can figure out what it is later." He looked around. "I think that's everything."

Beau snorted. "There's probably another room somewhere with a thousand more of these things. We need to get out of here. Baron Thomas could be talking to the abbot right now. He'll find out we're still here and come after us. We *have* to *leave*."

"Let's go," Kaye said.

We padded our way back up the stairs and through the darkness of the enormous library. I peeked out of the library door. No one was around. Clearly these monks took their silent meditation very seriously. Although considering how heartily they had all eaten, I had a feeling they were simply sleeping off their meal.

As we slid through the abbey doors into the chilly, starlit night, thinking about dinner made my gut give me a warning noise. "Kaye, Beau, I think I should get some food to take with us."

Still irritated with me for arguing with him in the placard room, Kaye said, "Fine. But hurry. And don't get caught. We're going to the stable to saddle our horses. We'll take them outside the abbey and wait for you in the trees across the road."

"Fine," I said right back to him. "I'll be there soon. Wait— what about Acorn?"

"We'll leave him here. The monks will take good care of him," Beau said.

"All right," I said. I walked around the abbey toward the gardens and found a kitchen door standing open to the night breeze. A lone monk snored in front of a dim fire. I found some bread and cheese from dinner, which went into my bag. Then I found piles of those delicious oatcakes heaped in a basket! I put plenty of them into my bag and left a few coins on a table for the snoring monk to find when he woke. I hoped it was enough.

I headed back to the gates of the abbey, and as I rounded the corner, I saw a cluster of six monks with torches. One of them looked very important—he was probably the abbot. What was even worse, he stood towering over Kaye and Beau with a grim face. I crouched behind a mounting block, trying to disappear into the darkness.

The abbot frowned, grasping Kaye's shoulder with a bony, powerful hand like a talon. He hissed loudly into Kaye's face, "I thought you might be trying to leave. You're wanted by the king for treason. I've been told to hold you prisoner until he has time to punish you appropriately. You'll pay for what you've done, make no mistake about that."

"King Aldric is a friend of mine," Kaye said, folding his arms across his chest. "I've committed no treason against him. And if you're saying that we've committed treason against Baron Thomas, let me remind you that he's no king of anything."

"Enough! He is not king yet, but he will be. The heavens have decreed it," the abbot growled, pushing Kaye ahead of him as he stalked across the yard, his long, vise-like fingers digging into Kaye's neck and shoulder. Two more monks seized Kaye's arms so he couldn't escape. "Bring the other one," the abbot called back to the other monks. They grabbed Beau and followed.

I cringed deeper into the shadows behind the mounting block as they passed. No one noticed me.

They skirted the garden and walked across a field until I could only see their silhouettes against the flickering light of their torches. They threw Kaye and Beau to the ground and my friends vanished. What had happened to them?

The monks returned, their sandals crunching on the gravel yard inside the abbey gates. "We'll leave them there until Baron Thomas can deal with them," the abbot said.

"I'm glad I'm not them," one of the monks said with a grin, baring his yellow teeth like a wolf. "Not now, and not when the baron gets his hands on them."

"Yes, well, I'd like to get my hands on them myself. They took the jewels and caused a serious setback in the baron's plot. Now he'll have to do something much smaller than he originally planned."

"The *baron's* plot?" the monk asked with a smirk.

"Yes, the baron's plot! But we will benefit from his pride and feelings of self-importance. This abbey was once celebrated throughout all of what is now Knox and Eldridge. It was the center of the kingdom. But when the country was divided, we became nothing but an old building tucked away in a corner of Eldridge, forgotten and ignored. We don't matter to anyone anymore. But we matter to the baron, and he will reward us generously when he is king."

"Why?" asked another monk.

"Because we've done more than he knows to help him become the ruler of Eldridge. Aldric is no imposter—despite what we've told the baron—but he's wasted too many opportunities to make this country rich and powerful. It is time for a new king. The baron will not make the same mistakes. So we will help him prove his claim to the throne, and he will not forget us when he becomes king."

The other monks nodded. As soon as they went inside the abbey, I dashed across the field to where Kaye and Beau had disappeared in the darkness.

CHapter eight

A warm, stinking odor rose up to meet me. I gagged and clapped a hand over my mouth. "Kaye! Beau! Are you here?"

"Yes." A muffled reply came from below my feet, floating upwards with another wave of stink.

"Don't come any farther; you'll fall in too," Kaye said in a nasal-sounding voice.

"You're in a pit! Are you all right? Why do you sound so funny?" I asked in a panic.

"We're breathing through our mouths," Beau explained.

I was doing the same thing myself. They were in the cesspit— the deep hole where the monks threw filth from the privies to decompose until it could be used to fertilize the gardens. From the smell, it had been filled recently.

"We can't climb out," Kaye said. "The sides are too steep, and they're slimy from the rain last night. We're up to our knees in filth."

"I'll find a rope," I said.

I dashed to the stables, watching out for the abbot and his bully monks. By now, the moon hung just above the trees, but inside the stable, all was dark.

My leg bumped against a soft, crackling bundle as I entered the stable, but I managed not to hurt myself. After blindly patting the walls, I found a coil of rope that seemed long enough. I ran back to the pit and lowered the rope to Kaye and Beau.

They climbed out, reeking of filth, their legs and arms coated with stinking, slippery mud.

"Ugh, you need a bath," I said.

Kaye glared at me. "It's your fault we got thrown in there, Reggie. You took so long we had to come back for you. That's when the abbot caught us."

"Be fair, Kaye," Beau said. "The abbot caught us because you left your bag of placards in the stable and you went back for it."

Kaye looked down and rubbed at his ear. "Well, that's true too. And I still refuse to leave the placards behind. I know they're important. Let's get them and get out of here!"

We found the bag of placards in the stable—it was the soft, crunchy thing I had bumped into earlier. Beau lingered in the stable to give Acorn a good-bye pat while I followed Kaye out of the stable and straight into Birket's arms.

"What are you doing here?" Birket said, his voice quavering with astonishment. "Fulkes, come out here!"

Fulkes emerged from the abbey to find Birket grasping me and Kaye by the backs of our shirts. "Oh-ho!" he said. "Are you running away? I thought the abbot threw you boys into the cesspit. How did you get out?"

Birket shook us until our teeth rattled and said, "I'm taking them straight to the baron. He'll deal with these two brats once and for all. They'll never be able to run away again when he's finished with them."

Kaye dropped the bag of placards. A few of them spilled onto the gravel. Fulkes picked one up. "What's this?" he began, but Birket interrupted with a scream as Kaye wiped his hand down the sticky leg of his pants, gathered a handful of brown goo, and swiped it across Birket's face.

Birket dropped both of us to wipe off his face and spit on the ground over and over. At the same moment, Beau barreled out of the stable and crashed into the soft part of Fulkes' stomach with his shoulder

"Oof!" Fulkes doubled over with a surprised grunt.

Kaye shouted, "Run!"and snatched up the bag of placards.

As we dashed out of the abbey and onto the main road I heard Birket say between spits, "There were three of them? I thought there were just two."

"After them!" Fulkes gasped. "They can't get far on foot. The baron will have our heads if they get away."

We sprinted across the road, leapt across a ditch, and crashed through the underbrush into the forest. Beau led us through the trees until we came to the clearing where our horses waited. Within seconds, we mounted our steeds and found the way back to the road.

Fulkes and Birket gaped at us as we sailed across the ditch and landed right in front of them.

"They have horses!" Fulkes screamed at Birket. "You idiot! Go get ours!"

I never heard Birket's response because our horses dashed away, their powerful hooves pounding the road as fast and loud as my heartbeats.

The road lay ahead of us, long and winding in the moonlight. Our horses thundered forward, the wind whooshing through their manes and flying up into my face. I felt like we galloped for hours, our horses' strides lengthening with every leap until it seemed like their feet no longer touched the ground.

"Don't fall asleep, Reggie," Beau shouted to me. "You'll fall off! Kaye, we need to rest the horses—and we need to rest Reggie too. I think we lost them."

We slowed the horses to a walk. Kaye and Beau smelled terrible. I tried to ride upwind of them, but we entered a forest and the trees blocked the night breezes from reaching us. Stench lingered around my friends like a sickly fog.

"We could sleep in the forest," I said.

Kaye agreed, but made us leave the road by walking the horses down the middle of a stream for a long way before allowing us to enter the forest.

After finding a hiding spot in the woods, we flopped down on the ground and fell asleep instantly, not even bothering to set a guard. I made sure to flop far away from Kaye and Beau so I wouldn't have to smell them in my sleep.

We woke to a chilly but clear morning and drank from the stream. Beau and Kaye washed the muck off their arms and legs as best they could. Then Kaye plunged his filthy face into the water and scrubbed at it with his hands. When he finished, he shook his hair and slicked it back, shivering from the icy water.

I noticed a scar on Kaye's forehead shaped like a tiny arrowhead. "How did you get that scar?" I asked as I passed around some food and we sat down to eat.

Kaye's face went dark. "When my father began training me to be a knight, I was terrible at it. He must have thought I would never be any good as a knight because he didn't even teach me to use a sword. Instead, he gave me exercises to make me good at jumping out of the way so I wouldn't get killed," he added with a sad smile.

"It's always better to jump out of the way than to get hurt," Beau said.

"My father doesn't jump out of the way," Kaye said. "He stands and fights like a real knight."

"You're a real knight," I said.

"I'm a real Sir Donkey," he said bitterly. "Anyway, my father also tried teaching me to jump off a fence onto Kadar's back— just one more way to run away—but I always fell. I practiced so hard, but weeks went by and I kept falling. Then one day, after watching me fail yet again, my father said I was jumping too small because I was afraid, but it wasn't keeping me safe. It was just giving me bruises. I needed to jump big, even if it felt too big."

"Did that help?" I asked.

Kaye nodded. "That night, when I practiced by myself, I jumped big. I jumped huge! I jumped so big I thought I would sail right over the horse, but it was just right and I landed on Kadar's back! I was so excited to show my father the next day."

"What did he say?" I asked.

"He never saw me do it. That morning, he gave me a new exercise—jumping back and forth and sideways over a shield on the ground. Then a king's messenger came, and my father went inside with him and left me alone all morning. I kept jumping until the noon meal. Afterward, when I tried to show my father how I could jump onto Kadar, my legs felt like jelly. They didn't work. I came crashing down worse than ever before. I hit my forehead on a stone and started bleeding everywhere."

Kaye's cheeks flushed with embarrassment. "I cried," he said. "I was only ten. My father held a cloth to my head and said I needed a break from training, that he had to go away for a while to Eldridge, but he'd help me again when he came back."

"And that's how you got that scar," I said.

"Yes," Kaye said. "But he never came back. I know he left because the king needed him here in Eldridge, but I'm the reason he won't come back. He knows I'll never be a knight like him. I'll only ever be Sir Donkey."

"Your father's proud of you," Beau said.

Kaye shrugged. "If I can't find out what kind of danger he's in, he'll die, and he'll die disappointed in me. I need to save him, but I need to save him like a real knight would—like my father would, like a hero." Kaye stood up. "So let's go to Kingsbridge and find Azam. He'll tell us about the baron's plan."

We returned to the road, and seeing no sign of Fulkes and Birket, we rode hard, reaching Kingsbridge by early afternoon. It was a port city, perched right on the ocean and busy with merchants and guildsmen and sailors, all rushing about their business, as well as lots of idle men lounging and gaming in squares and on doorsteps. Gulls cried overhead as Kaye began asking for the Pigpenny Inn in Cotswold Lane. After a few wrong turns, we found the inn. A funny sign hung over the door showing a big penny with a smiling pig on it.

"I'll find a stable that will keep our horses safe," Beau said, taking our reins and preparing to lead the horses away. "You two find Azam."

Kaye entered the inn. A rowdy crew of hungry customers sat at tables around a fire. A woman brought them black bread and bowls of soup that looked like cabbage water with a few strings of meat floating on top.

As she passed by, Kaye waved and called out to her, "Can you help me, please?"

She flashed us a cheerful grin across her tray. "Business is booming. There's plenty of men in town with nothing to do but fill their bellies. What do you want, boys?" she bellowed.

"I'm looking for Azam," Kaye yelled.

She looked confused. "You're looking for a what?"

"Azam—a man. He lives here. He has one hand," Kaye hollered, standing on his toes so he could put strength into his yell.

"Oh, why didn't you say so? Upstairs. Third door on the left. Unless he's out. I'm coming, I'm coming," she yelled to the waiting men.

Upstairs, Kaye knocked on Azam's door.

"Do you hear anything?" I asked.

He shook his head and knocked again, pressing his ear to the door. "It's too loud downstairs."

Kaye knocked a third time. The door flew open and Kaye stumbled into the room, almost treading on the feet of Azam, the one-handed jeweler. Azam wore a long-sleeved tunic with one sleeve folded and stitched over the space where his hand used to be.

"Who are you?" he asked with a frown, crinkling his forehead so tightly that his eyebrows met in the middle. "What do you mean by knocking on my door over and over again?"

CHAPTER NINE

"I'm sorry," Kaye said. "It's so loud downstairs I couldn't hear you."

The man smiled, the creases around his eyes warming the expression on his tired face. "I'll shut the door so we can hear each other now," he said.

Azam gestured for us to sit on the bed. He sat on a stool near a good-sized table covered with books of numbers written in neat columns and rows. A small window looked down a street to the harbor, where boats floated at rest in the bay.

"Are you Azam?" Kaye asked.

"Yes. Who are you?" he asked suspiciously.

"I'm Kaye—um, Sir Kaye, from Knox. You told one of the gem-carving prisoners that my father—Sir Henry—and the king of Eldridge are in danger. I need to save them, but first I need to know what the danger is. I hoped you would help me."

"But I am powerless to help anyone, even myself," Azam said.

An uncomfortable silence fell over the room as Kaye stared intently at Azam. I had to say something! "Where are you from?" I asked.

Azam looked at me and smiled. "I come from the south countries, where I was known for my skill at cutting and polishing gems. Above all else, I was famous for carving gems with beautiful designs of leaves and flowers."

I nodded. "Why did you come to Eldridge?"

A small frown settled between his eyebrows. "After I lost my hand, I couldn't work or take care of my family. Then I heard of a man in Eldridge who needed someone to teach others to carve gems. So I packed up my family and we came."

Kaye finally spoke. "You brought your family with you?"

I glanced around the room. There was no sign of a family here. There was nothing here. "Where are they?" I asked.

Azam dropped his face to his hand. "They are taken. Imagine how I felt when I arrived and learned that the baron wished me to travel to Knox and instruct prisoners. At first, I was happy to do so. If they learned a new skill, they could work when they left prison. But then I learned that the men were not imprisoned for committing crimes. They had been kidnapped—taken from their families without a chance to even say good-bye or let their families know they were alive!"

"We freed them, you know," I whispered. "They've all gone home to their families by now."

Azam patted my head. "You are good boys. You did what I couldn't, no matter how much I wanted to. Your parents must be very proud of you."

"Maybe," Kaye said faintly.

With a smile, Azam said, "Surely they are. No family should be parted by force. It is truly a noble deed to reunite such deserving ones."

"Yes, it is," Kaye said.

Azam ran his hand through his short black hair and added, "Later, I was even more distressed to discover that the jewels my students carved were meant to pay an army to conquer the king of my new home. When I learned this, it was enough! I told Baron Thomas, 'No! I refuse to be part of this any longer.'"

"What happened?" I asked.

"He took my family. My wife, Samir, and my little girl, Melita. He took them away and said I must do everything he asked of me or they would come to great harm."

"Where are they?" I asked, horrified.

He pointed out the window. "On a boat called the *Triumph*. It docks once a month for supplies. Sometimes Baron Thomas lets me go aboard and see them. They're locked in the ship's cabin. The captain is a great friend of Baron Thomas, and he wears the key to the cabin around his neck at all times—to keep my family safe, he says."

"When will you see them again?" I asked, keeping the conversation going. Kaye had gone back to being silent.

He shrugged. "The boat will probably dock tonight, but because Baron Thomas is gone, I won't see my family until next month. Perhaps longer."

"That's not fair," I said. "Baron Thomas is a cruel man. Is he really the true king?" I asked.

Azam shrugged. "He *is* of royal blood. He's a descendant of King Aethelfred's youngest son, but Aldric descends from the oldest twin and the kingship has always belonged to that line. The baron could possibly take the kingship from Aldric if enough of the nobles of Eldridge supported him." He frowned. "A great many of them do support him."

I asked something I had been curious about for a long time. "What do you do for Baron Thomas now that you're not teaching prisoners?"

Azam pointed to the open books on the table. "I'm in charge of his money. I have the key to his warehouse near the docks, and I run his business. He's a wool merchant."

"Oh," I said, surprised. "So is my father. He—"

Kaye interrupted. "Please, Azam, tell me how he plans to kill the king and my father," Kaye begged. "I must save them."

Azam bowed his head and said, "I'm sorry, I can't. My first duty is to my family. I must keep them safe at any price—even at the cost of the lives of two good men."

Kaye looked wonderingly at Azam. "I wish my father were more like you," he said. "He left us and came here because other people were more important than we were. He always puts duty ahead of everything." With tightened lips, Kaye added, "Sometimes I wish he would forget about duty and put his family first. I miss him."

I stared at Kaye. I had never, *ever* heard him admit that his father was anything less than perfect.

Azam put his good hand on Kaye's shoulder. "His coming has been a great blessing to both countries. He's done great things here, but I promise you, it was not easy for him to leave you. I am a father. I know."

Kaye shrugged and said, "Well, if I'm going to be just like him, I have to do what he would do. A knight must help the helpless. I will rescue your wife and daughter when the boat docks tonight, if you can be ready to leave with them. Take them to Knox and the queen will help you."

Azam blinked. "But—but you are a child. You can't put yourself in such danger. Baron Thomas is a powerful enemy, and he already hates you."

A hard expression fell over Kaye's face. "If he kills my father, I'll lose any chance of ever having my family together again. Let me try to save your family. It's what my father would do."

"Kaye, if you don't agree with everything your father does, why must you be just like him?" Azam asked.

"Because he's the perfect knight," Kaye replied with a small smile and a shrug.

I felt sad for Kaye. There were many things about my own father that I didn't agree with—his passion for money and his obsession with wool, the way he embarrassed himself trying to impress rich people, and most of all, his constant disappointment in me because I was so slow to learn things. I couldn't imagine disliking all these things about my father and still trying to be just like him.

Kaye sat up straight. "I will rescue your family tonight," he said firmly. "Where can we meet you?"

Azam pointed out the window. "See the house with the red roof—a friend lives there. I'll be there by last bells tonight." He shook his head. "I can't believe you're doing this. It's too dangerous. You're only children."

"That's good," I said. "No one expects boys to be doing anything important."

"Baron Thomas might," Azam said. "Fulkes and Birket came here earlier today. The baron sent them after you. He believes you took something from the abbey that belongs to him. Fulkes and Birket think you're going to Rombauer Castle to meet your father, so if you are going that way, be careful. They'll take you to the baron and he will not be kind."

I stiffened in my seat. "We only have placards," I said. "He must really want them back."

"And we're not going to Rombauer Castle—at least not yet." Kaye said. "We're staying here to rescue your family from the baron first."

"Fulkes and Birket are staying here too," Azam said. "They're sleeping in the stable behind the baron's warehouse tonight because there's nowhere to stay in the city. The town is full of men. At the inns, people sleep three to a bed and on the tables and floors—even in the stables. Remember that army Baron Thomas wanted to hire?"

"Yes," Kaye said, sounding confused.

"They're here. They're waiting for the baron to return and organize them into an army—but what they really want is their pay. Without the jewels, the baron can't pay them, so he's heading to Rombauer City now, staying far away from the men."

"The baron doesn't have any other money?" I asked.

Azam shook his head. "Hardly any. He's a wool merchant. His warehouse is full of wool, not money. He's keeping it until the price is highest, and then he'll sell."

Kaye stood up, "Thank you. We'll see you tonight."

"Why are you helping me?" Azam asked. "I never promised you the information you want. You don't know if I'll help you at all in return for my family."

Kaye looked Azam straight in the eyes. "Your family deserves help. I will help them. A man I respect once told me that you're a good man who can be trusted. I don't need to know more than that."

Azam stood up, bending at the waist to Kaye. "You are a noble soul, Sir Kaye, and a fine knight in your own way—no matter who your father is."

"My father is Sir Henry," Kaye said with a solemn face, "and I must live up to his name."

"Perhaps, in time, your name will surpass his," Azam said as he opened the door.

"Oh, no," Kaye said. "But maybe I will make him proud someday."

Azam laid his hand on Kaye's head. "That day has already come, Sir Kaye. May heaven go with you on your noble quest."

Kaye marched down the stairs, never looking back.

chapter ten

We waited in front of the inn for Beau, who came up the street whistling a tune. "Our horses will be safe until we need them," he said. "Did you find Azam?"

"Yes." Kaye stood up. "I think he'll tell us what we need to know, but first we have to rescue his wife and daughter. They're prisoners on a ship called the *Triumph.*"

We strolled through the streets until we found a market square where we wouldn't be noticed. Children ran shouting across it, and a few men sitting around the edges played at dice games. Women stood in clusters, chattering together like birds. Two pigs ambled through the square, grunting good-naturedly.

We sat down under a tree and Kaye explained his plan. "The ship will dock tonight for supplies. That's our only chance to rescue Azam's family. They're locked in the cabin, and the captain wears the key around his neck."

"How will we get the key?" I asked.

"We need to know the captain's habits—where he goes when he comes to shore and what he likes to do. One of us needs to go down to the docks, ask around, and find out more about the captain."

"I suppose you want me to do it," I said. "What should I do?"

"There are plenty of alehouses by the docks," Beau suggested. "People in alehouses like to talk."

"Fine," I said. "Where will I find you again?"

"We'll be right here," Kaye said. "Try to hurry."

I headed downhill toward the bay. The docks swarmed with people, reminding me of clusters of bees climbing up and down their hives.

Alehouses seemed to sprout up around the docks in circles, just like mushrooms in a patch of grass. Sailors must be very thirsty people.

I stepped inside the first alehouse I saw, looked around, and backed out again. It was a loud, busy place, and I would never get anyone's attention in there. I wandered down one of the docks instead and found some boys watching a ship come in.

I nodded to one and he nodded back. He seemed friendly. "What's that ship?" I asked.

"*The Rose of Eldridge*, of course. It's His Majesty's most powerful warship. It's a cog ship. See the high sides? That makes it harder for enemies to board it, but easier for the sailors on *The Rose* to board other ships and take them. Archers can shoot from that high part too."

I looked at the boy with respect. "You know a lot about ships."

He nodded, looking pleased. "There's nothing I don't know about ships. My father and my uncle are both sailors. Someday I will be too. My name's Theo."

"I'm Reggie." I pointed to the *Triumph*. "Is that one of His Majesty's ships?"

He looked where I was pointing and laughed. "Naw," he said. "That's old Captain Claymore's cog ship. He's a merchant. He sails up and down the coast, buying goods in one port and selling them in another. When he's not doing that, he lives on his boat in this bay."

"Would he ever hire a boy on his ship?" I asked.

Theo snorted. "All the time. But you don't want to sail with Captain Claymore. He's not a careful captain. Boys on his ship fall overboard or get drowned or hit in the head with a spar. If you want a job, you can get one on the docks. They always need hands to load and unload ships. They'll even hire you for an hour or two if you just need a few coins."

"I'd rather be a sailor," I said.

"Well, Captain Claymore is due for supplies. He'll be ashore tonight. You could talk to him then."

"Do I go to the ship?" I asked.

"No, he always goes straight to the Swann bathhouse when he lands. You can wait for him outside. He's usually in a good mood after a bath. Then he goes to the alehouse. You'll never get a sensible word out of him after that."

"How will I know him?" I asked.

Theo shrugged. "He wears a funny hat. And he likes to be left alone. That's why he lives on his boat."

Theo showed me the Swann bathhouse and left me there. The sign above the door showed a white swan in a nest. Underneath, it said "Men's Bathhouse." Now I needed to find my way back to the square, but I couldn't even remember how to get back to the docks! What if it took me all night to find my friends again? When I turned around, my heart pounding, I almost fainted with relief when I saw Kaye and Beau walking toward me.

"What are you doing here?" I asked.

Kaye shrugged, but Beau said, "Kaye was worried about you. We remembered you get lost easily, so we followed you. What did you learn?"

"That it's easy to get a job at the docks loading and unloading ships, and the *Triumph* should be docking for supplies soon.

After it docks, Captain Claymore comes straight to this bath-house for his monthly bath. Then he goes to an alehouse and drinks all night."

"Can you get a job helping to load supplies onto the *Triumph*, Beau?" Kaye asked.

"Yes, I'm sure they'll be glad of another pair of arms."

"Good," Kaye said. "While you do that, Reggie and I will get the key from the captain while he's in his bath. Then we'll come find you and figure out the rest of the plan together."

I followed Kaye to a market square that glowed with golden sunset light. Kaye found a junk dealer, and after poking through a pile of odd and ends, he bought four keys. Then he led us back to the Swann like an arrow flying to the target—as easily as if he had lived in this city all his life.

Inside the Swann, a bearded man sat in a small room, in front of another door leading farther inside the building.

"I'm Abel Swann, owner of this respected bathhouse," he said.

"How much for a bath, good sir?" Kaye asked.

Abel Swann flicked a glance at him. "More than you can pay, youngling. This is the finest bathhouse in Kingsbridge with the best food and the cleanest water. Go somewhere else for a bath, boy."

"Please," Kaye begged. "Some monks threw me in a cesspit. I can't stand my smell."

The man looked up in surprise but he shook his head. "You'll do better elsewhere, boy. Get along with you. I'm expecting some real customers soon. It's almost time for the evening meal."

Outside again, Kaye headed to the back of the building. "We'll just creep inside and hide until the captain shows up. When he gets undressed, we'll get the key," he said.

"Where are you going to hide, Kaye? Underwater?"

"No," he said. "There's got to be somewhere in there where we can hide *and* breathe." He stashed his cloak behind a nearby barrel and opened the bathhouse door. A puff of steamy air came out to meet us. I left my cloak with Kaye's and we stepped inside.

Long wooden tubs lined with linen sheets filled a big room. Wooden trays stretched across the tubs. A few men lounged in the tubs, soaking and chatting. Two of them sat in the water and played at a game of draughts set on one of the wooden trays. Others ate meals while soaking in the water. Although several of the men wore hats while sitting there, none of the hats could be described as funny.

"Captain Claymore isn't here yet," I said to Kaye as I followed him farther into the room. We walked like we belonged there, and no one paid any attention to us.

Several young women and boys ran back and forth between the tubs, carrying trays of food and buckets of steaming water. One man yelped as a boy poured a fresh bucket of hot water into his tub.

"Careful, boy, I came here to bathe, not to be boiled alive!" he cried out.

"Sorry, sir, sorry," the boy muttered, backing away. As soon as the man took his eyes off him, the boy scuttled away and soon reappeared with another bucket of hot water. Someone beckoned to him, and he ran over to that tub and added the hot water before picking up a brush and scrubbing at that man's back.

The man handed the boy a coin and stood up. I cringed, not wanting to see any more of him, but to my surprise, he wore a short leather apron around his waist to protect his modesty.

I sighed with relief, but just then the front door opened and Abel Swann entered the room. The bathers called out greetings and compliments on the hot baths and food.

"Quick, in here," Kaye said, pulling open a small door. We popped inside and shut the door behind us.

CHAPTER ELEVEN

We stood in a small room with a large tub of steaming water in the middle of it. A screen between the door and the tub protected the tub from drafts. Behind another screen in the corner, we saw a peg on the wall for hanging up clothes. In the middle of the wall, a small fire smoldered in a fireplace, while a large bundle of fresh herbs and a brush rested on a stool near the tub.

As the door opened again, we ducked behind the screen and heard Abel Swann say, "Here's your private bath, Captain Claymore. Please call if you need anything."

The door shut and we found ourselves face to face with Captain Claymore. He was a large man and he did wear a funny hat—it looked like a tall stocking, with the top fitting over his head and the long leg of the stocking wrapped around his head a few times like a turban.

"This is a private bath. Get out." The captain stomped behind the screen and threw his coat on the floor in a heap, exactly the way my mother had always told me not to.

Kaye didn't blink. "Captain Claymore, we're your personal attendants today. If there's anything you need, we can help you."

He grunted. "Then scent the bath and fetch my dinner."

Kaye gestured at the herbs near the bath. "Crumple them up into the water," he murmured. "I'll bring the food."

I grabbed the bundle of greenery, tore it into bits and sprinkled it in the tub. A warm breath of steam rose from the water and hit my face with the sharp scent of lavender and the honeyed odor of chamomile. I knew these herbs. My mother kept them in her kitchen to make poultices and medicines. I thought of my mother and her fondness for me. Then I thought of my father and felt the sharp pang that pierced my heart whenever he looked at me with disappointment.

"Stop dawdling, boy. Help me with the tub," Captain Claymore snapped. "If you were on my ship, you'd pay attention when I speak or I'd whip some respect into you. You'll never get anywhere in life if you spend the day dreaming like that."

I glanced at him in surprise and said, "That's what my father always says."

"He's right. Listen to him."

The captain stood there waiting, his hairy belly hanging over his little leather apron. I stuck my finger in the water and said, "I think it's just right. It shouldn't burn you now."

When the captain climbed over the high side of the tub, I realized the apron only covered him in front. His belly wasn't the only hairy thing about him. His backside looked like a bear's backside. I knew that for a fact. I had met a bear not too long ago.

Captain Claymore settled into the tub. The herbs floated to the top, so he looked like he was sitting in a puddle of fresh-mown hay. He still wore his ridiculous hat.

Kaye returned, carrying a tray of food and a board, which he placed across the tub, filling it with roasted meat and bread and boiled eggs in fish sauce and broiled fish in wine sauce, and a large, flat wedge of soft cheese oozing out of its chalky-looking rind.

Captain Claymore barked out one word. "Wine!"

"I'll get it," Kaye said.

I gazed around wildly, looking for something to do. The dying fire caught my eye, so I pulled sticks of wood from a nearby stack and built up the blaze bit by bit. I darted a glance at Captain Claymore's neck. Sure enough, a good-sized key hung from a thin leather strap.

Now I knew why Kaye had bought those keys at the junk stall. He wanted to swap out a fake key for the real one so Captain Claymore wouldn't know it was missing. I hoped Kaye had a brilliant idea for making the switch, because I sure didn't.

When Kaye reappeared with the wine, I pointed at the captain's neck. Kaye winked. I guess he did have a plan.

What he actually had was a knife.

When Captain Claymore finished, Kaye took away everything but the wine and the oozy cheese and bread. Moments later, he brought back two buckets of steaming water.

"I brought more hot water, Captain," he said. "I'll warm your bath and scrub your back."

The captain grunted and closed his eyes. Kaye poured hot water into the tub, making sure not to splash the captain. Then he scrubbed the captain's shaggy back. The captain leaned forward, his head coming to rest on the tray across his tub. The key also landed on the tray, its leather cord drooping slackly towards the water.

Kaye moved the brush back and forth, back and forth, around and around in a hypnotic motion. The captain began to snore. Kaye waved me over and transferred the brush to my hand, making a signal for me to keep moving the brush.

Then Kaye pulled a knife out of his pocket. With a stealthy hand, he lifted a fraction of the leather string from around the captain's neck and darted the blade across it. The leather broke, and leaving the key resting on the tray-table, right under Captain Claymore's open mouth, Kaye cautiously pulled the leather string out of the key and off the captain's neck.

With a hard stare, he sized up the real key and found one of his junk keys with a similar size and shape. Sliding the leather string through the new key, he carefully cut the old knot off

the string and knotted it together again with the new key on it. It looked almost exactly like the old necklace, except that the captain's greasy head was missing from the middle of it.

Kaye pointed to the real key. He wanted me to get it. I gingerly reached around the captain's head to where the key rested on the tray. His snoring mouth was only three fingers' breadth above the key. I hooked one finger over the key, dragging it toward the edge of the tray, where I could safely grab it without touching the captain's face. I pulled the key out and held it up to show Kaye.

After a moment, I realized the liquid dripping from the key wasn't water, but the captain's own foul-scented drool. I made a face and dunked the key in the second bucket of water before drying it on my clothes and putting it in my pocket.

"How are you going to get that back over his head?" I asked.

"I won't," he breathed into my ear. It tickled and made me squirm. "He'll do it himself."

Kaye grabbed the leather string with both hands, searched for a weak spot, and yanked at it until the leather broke.

"What are you doing?" I whispered in open-mouthed horror.

Kaye held the broken necklace in one hand. With the other, he shook Captain Claymore's shoulder. "I'll rinse your back now, Captain."

"What? Oh, yes, yes, rinse my back now," the captain mumbled.

Kaye lifted the second bucket and poured a drenching torrent over the captain's shoulders. The curly black hairs on his back turned into perfectly straight lines in that gushing river of hot water.

At the same time, Kaye dropped the necklace into the captain's lap. It hit the water with a soft plop and disappeared beneath the floating blanket of herbs.

"Oh, Captain, I'm so sorry," he said. "The cord around your neck broke. You'd best find it if you don't want to lose it."

The captain clapped a hand to his chest and then fumbled in the water until he pulled up the soaking leather cord and key. He knotted the cord and placed it around his neck with a grunt.

"Good as new," he said. "The knot will tighten as it dries."

"Do you want more hot water?" Kaye asked. "If not, we'll leave you alone to soak."

"No, no, it's hot enough. Go away. There's nowhere a man can get any peace anymore—not even in his bath."

"Good night, Captain," Kaye said. We left the room and wound our ways separately through the rows of tubs to the back door. Twilight had fallen while we were inside the bathhouse.

"I can't believe you did that!" I said, breathing deeply of the chilly night air. It felt refreshing after the close steaminess of the bathhouse. "How did you get the food and water and wine for him?"

"Oh, that was easy," Kaye said. "I went to the kitchen and told them I was taking care of the captain this evening. They thought I came with him."

"And he thought you came with the bath!" I said with a snort of laughter.

Kaye found our cloaks where we had left them and together we ran like greyhounds toward the docks, never even noticing the two men watching us from the open door of an alehouse.

chapter twelve

We crouched behind some barrels and crates on the dock, watching workers carry boxes to and from the *Triumph*. Already, chests and barrels of fresh supplies made a small mountain in the middle of the boat.

"Look, there's Beau," Kaye said.

Beau was helping a man lift a heavy barrel from the dock up to two other men inside the ship. He had gotten taller lately. In the dim light, he looked just like one of the men.

"How are we going to get his attention?" I asked.

"Easy," Kaye said.

I thought he'd have a big plan involving signals and disguises, but he just walked up to Beau and tapped him on the shoulder. "Can you help me with something?" he asked.

Beau shrugged and followed Kaye. "I'll be right back," he told the other men.

Kaye led him back to me and said, "See? Easy."

I laughed, even though I didn't want to.

"Now we'll make our plan," Kaye said. "Beau, can you find out where Azam's family is being kept?"

"There's only one locked door on the ship. You can see it from here." He pointed to a door near the pile of supplies. "They'll be in there. Trust me. I've been through the entire ship several times already. There's nowhere else they could possibly be except inside that door."

"Good," Kaye said. "You need to unlock that door, let Azam's family out, and take them behind that pile of supplies. No one will see them back there. Everyone's working on the dock side of the ship, right?"

"Yes," Beau said, "but everyone will see them leave the cabin. There's nowhere to hide between the cabin and the pile."

"Then we'll need a distraction," Kaye decided.

"I could yell for help," I said.

Beau shook his head. "It needs to be something big. Something people fear."

"Not another pretend monster," I said, thinking of the trick we had played on the guards at the manor house back in Knox.

"No," Beau said. "Something real this time. Something everyone fears. Fire."

Startled, we looked at Beau. He pointed to a pile of wooden boxes and barrels stacked near us. "Those are empty, and they're filled with old straw to cushion the supplies that used to be inside them. The straw will burn easily, and then the boxes will burn. Everyone will rush to put the fire out."

"Great idea, Beau," Kaye said, his face full of excitement at the idea of setting something on fire for a good cause. "So, once everyone is distracted, Beau, you let Samir and Melita out of the cabin, hide them behind the pile of supplies, and help them climb down the other side of the ship, where I will be waiting in a rowboat. Then I'll row them to safety."

"Wait a minute," I said. "If you're in the rowboat and Beau's on the ship, where am I?"

"You have to set the fire," Kaye said.

"What if I get caught?" I said. "These docks are wood. They'll burn. These ships are wood. They'll burn. They're valuable ships.

Lots of them belong to the king. I could be severely punished. I could be whipped or even branded."

"It's up to you," Kaye said. "Someone has to set the fire. And someone has to be in the boat. What are you better at? Lighting fires or rowing?"

I looked at the ground. I couldn't row. I'd never been in a boat in my life. "Lighting fires," I said in a low voice.

"So you'll do it?" Kaye asked. "Please? This is important. We're running out of time to save my father." His eyes looked desperate.

"I'll do it," I said.

Kaye threw an arm over my shoulders and said, "Thanks, Reggie. Now we need to borrow a rowboat. I'll row myself up beside the ship and call out to you, Beau. When you hear me, signal Reggie to start the distraction."

"Good," Beau said. "Reggie, when it's time to start the distraction, I'll stand in front of the pile and wipe my brow like this." He demonstrated.

"I'll be watching," I said. I handed Beau the captain's key.

We made plans to meet in a square near the church with the highest steeple in Kingsbridge if we got separated. Beau went back to work. Together, Kaye and I found a lonely rowboat tied to another dock. Kaye climbed into it and rowed toward the *Triumph*.

I ran back to the pile of empty boxes, crouched behind it, and stared at Beau so hard I thought my eyes would break. I didn't want to miss the signal and ruin everything.

While I waited, I worried about what might happen if the fire got out of control. What would I write down in my Royal Chronicles of Knox? Probably something like this: "Beau released the prisoners, Kaye rowed them to safety, and Reggie accidentally burned down the entire city of Kingsbridge."

I sighed, but I brightened up when I thought that if I did burn down the city, I probably wouldn't have to write down any of our adventures after all. We'd already had so many that I'd be a hundred years old before I finished writing them down, because I wrote so slowly and so badly. I felt embarrassed at the thought of anyone seeing a book written by me.

I blinked. Beau stood in front of the supplies, wiping his brow with a dramatic gesture. I pulled the flint and tinder from my bag, quickly sparked a glowing speck to life, and began feeding it scraps of fuel.

The spark became a tiny flame, slowly eating the bits of shredded cloth I gave it. Then it grew stronger and it could manage one of the packing straws from the crate. I gave it another. Suddenly it took on a life of its own, grabbing its own food with greedy, fiery fingers.

All at once, the entire bundle of straw inside the crate was burning. Then the fire seized the crate itself and spread to the straw in the next one.

I ran away, barely managing to hide myself before someone shouted, "Fire!" All the men abandoned their work to put out the fire, which spread through the pile of garbage much faster than I had expected.

Meanwhile, Beau unlocked the captain's door, brought out a woman and child, and relocked the door. They vanished behind the pile of supplies.

When I saw Beau hop down off the ship with a bucket and begin dipping up seawater to help with the fire, I knew Samir and Melita were safe in the boat with Kaye. Within moments,

the fire was gone. I sighed with relief. I wouldn't be responsible for burning down the city after all.

When people had calmed down and gone back to their homes or ships or alehouses with a fine story to tell, I dashed back along the dock to the shore. I spotted Kaye tying up the rowboat where we had found it. He tried to help Samir out of the boat, but the little girl made it difficult by clinging to her mother's neck, her tiny arms wrapped as tight as a hangman's noose. I ran to help and between the two of us, we got them safely ashore.

As we turned toward the town, I saw Fulkes and Birket leaning heavily against the corner of a building. They saw us at the same time.

"I told you! I knew it was them when I heard there was a fire. I bet they tried to burn down the baron's warehouse!" Birket screeched.

Fulkes lunged toward Kaye face-first, like a dog after a squirrel, shouting, "Ho there! You! Sir Donkey! Come here!"

CHAPTER THIRTEEN

Kaye and I pulled Samir into the crowded main street that ran uphill, away from the docks. We'd meet Beau later. First we needed to lose Fulkes and Birket in the crowd.

Men with angry faces filled the street. As we ran, I heard them grumble, "Who does he think he is, making us wait for our money?" and, "Where is this baron anyway? Shouldn't he be here by now?"

No matter how fast we ran, Fulkes and Birket were right behind us. Poor Samir struggled to carry Melita and keep running. All those months of being stuck on a boat made her legs weak and unsteady on land.

Fulkes charged up the hill, head down and arms pumping, panting hard. Birket ran more easily than Fulkes and seemed to be chasing after me, not Kaye or Samir. He reached out his bony arm, and managed to grab the corner of my shoulder with his knobby fingers.

"I have you now!" he said. "The baron will be so happy to meet you and Sir Donkey. You stole his jewels and his placards—and now you tried to burn down his warehouse! You're his personal enemies now!"

Seeing that Birket had me, Fulkes slowed to a steady jog.

"I don't have anything!" I shouted, running even harder. Birket matched my speed easily, still holding onto my shoulder. "Let me go!"

"Never!" Birket shrieked, blasting me with his hot, ale-scented breath. "You're worth your weight in gold to me. That's how much the baron will pay me for bringing you to him!"

"Baron Thomas has no gold, you fool!" I shouted. "He can't pay you anything. His gems are gone! He can't even pay that army he hired. That's why he's not here. He's hiding in Rombauer City. All he has left is wool. Am I worth my weight in wool to you?"

Momentarily stumped, but still running and holding onto my shoulder, Birket paused to think that one over. At the same time, several of the angry-faced men turned to look at us. One of them cried out, "What's all this about Baron Thomas not being able to pay? He promised us money!"

Birket gasped as he realized I had just spoiled the baron's secret, and while he was distracted, I ducked with a sudden twist and sank my teeth into his hand. With a sharp cry, he lost his hold on my shoulder, stumbling over his long legs as I got away.

I ran uphill, searching for Kaye and Samir, but I couldn't find them anywhere. I saw Birket gaining on me again, although this time a small group of men followed him, pelting him with questions.

I dove through the nearest open door into a crowded alehouse. Rolling under a table, I scurried on all fours through a maze of table legs and human legs, trying to find a way out. Spying a door, I leaped to my feet and ran for it, vanishing into the back room of the alehouse, where I found another door leading to an alley. I loped downhill through the alley, and soon found an opening between buildings that led back to the main road.

I peered around a corner of a building, looking for Fulkes and Birket, but I didn't see anything. I stood just a few paces from the docks. I knew how to find our meeting place from here!

I found the tall-steepled church where Kaye and Beau waited for me. Samir's smooth, dark hair gleamed in the moonlight shining down into the quiet square. The little girl curled her face into Samir's neck, so I couldn't see her, but I could tell she had her thumb in her mouth.

"You made it!" Kaye said. "I was worried you'd get lost."

"Me too," I said. "What happened?"

"Samir and I hid while you were, um, distracting Birket," Kaye said, looking guilty. "Then when Fulkes and Birket passed us, we came here to wait for you. I'm sorry we left you, but I had to get Samir away. She couldn't run any longer."

With a shock, I realized that Kaye had deliberately left me behind. I swallowed a big gulp of air that felt like a sharp-edged bubble behind my breastbone. "But what if I hadn't gotten away?" I asked.

"I was sure you would," Kaye said, but he didn't meet my eyes.

"But I might not have," I said.

"Then we would have had to rescue you too," Beau said.

Kaye didn't say anything. I started to wonder if he would have rescued me. Kaye only had two days to get to the king's castle and save his father's life. He protected Samir because it was his duty, and her safety meant that Azam would tell Kaye the details about the baron's plan to kill the king and Sir Henry. My safety wouldn't help rescue Sir Henry. Whose life was more important? Mine or Sir Henry's? I knew the answer already, and the pain in my chest tightened. Sir Henry's life was the most important thing to him now.

Kaye led us through a maze of quiet streets to the house with the red roof. I was glad to follow. As soon as we left the square, I was hopelessly lost. I kept imagining Birket behind me, ready to pounce, but when I turned around, I didn't see anything. The dark streets all looked identically unfriendly to me, full of mysterious shadows and whispers and footsteps just out of sight and just out of hearing. It gave me shivers that wouldn't stop, no matter how tightly I wrapped my cloak around me.

I felt better when we reached the safety of the red-roofed house. An older woman let us in and embraced Samir, murmuring, "I thought I'd never see you again."

Azam threw his arms around his wife and daughter, weeping openly. "I never should have brought you here," he said. "I have hated myself every day for doing this to you. I should have thought only of your safety."

"You could not have known," Samir said, through her own happy tears. "How I have missed you!"

"And I have missed you," Azam said. "But we must leave. Our punishment will be terrible if the baron catches us." Turning to Kaye, he said, "I fear for you. Come with us to the safety of Knox."

Kaye stood up very straight and said, "My father would never run away to safety. Neither will I. If Baron Thomas kills my father and the king, it will surely lead to war between Knox and Eldridge. How can I stop him?"

Azam handed Kaye a sheet of parchment and a key. "You will find what you need to know in here. Thank you for my family, Kaye. I wish the best for you."

"What happened to your hand?" Samir asked, lifting Kaye's left hand. A splotch of fresh blood spread across his tattered bandage. Blisters, burst and ragged, lined the rest of both his hands, leaving oozing raw spots that made my own hands sting just looking at them.

"Oh, Kaye, we forgot about your hand!" I said with regret. "I should have rowed the boat."

Kaye shrugged. "You didn't know how. So I did it. We saved Samir. That's all that matters."

The sharp bubble inside my chest softened a bit. Knowing that Kaye had hurt himself while rescuing Samir made me feel a little better about Kaye leaving me behind. He put duty first and did what he must to save her.

Samir put a hand on Kaye's cheek and leaned down to kiss the other one. "I thank you, my brave knight. You saved our lives at the cost of your own skin."

Kaye blushed. "Thank you, my lady. You do me honor."

"Come," Azam said. "I have horses. We must leave now." He picked up a heavy pack and he and his family went out into the darkness alone.

CHapteR fourteeN

After Azam and his family departed, Odessa, the widow who owned the house, put fresh bandages on Kaye's hands. She gave us food and blankets and then settled us by her fire.

"Sleep well, you've earned it," she said, climbing a ladder to the loft where she slept. "You did good work tonight, reuniting a family so cruelly split apart."

Kaye sat by the fire with Azam's note and read aloud, "Baron Thomas plans to murder King Aldric and frame your father for his death so that Eldridge will declare war against Knox. Then the baron will arrest and kill your father in punishment for the king's death. With King Aldric gone, Baron Thomas plans to take the throne himself and lead Eldridge to conquer Knox. His dearest wish is to unite the two countries once more under his own rule, just as they were united under King Aethelfred long ago.

"Baron Thomas plans to do this on King Aethelfred's Day of Remembrance. On that day, your father and King Aldric will perform a jousting display with blunt lances, but Fulkes and Birket have orders to drug the king with syrup of poppies in wine so he will be too sleepy to fight. The king will also be given a beautiful blue and gold lance, but this lance will be damaged so it will break upon impact.

"Fulkes and Birket will give your father a plain lance with a fatally sharp steel tip hidden under a blunt cover. During the joust, he will injure and possibly kill the king—if he doesn't, Baron Thomas' men will kill the king themselves, under the guise of 'helping' him after his fall.

"This is all I know about the baron's plan. But I have taken all of Baron Thomas' remaining money and given it to the poor this very day. He will find it very difficult to accomplish his lofty goals with no money to pay his supporters. We shall see how loyal they are to him then."

"What is the key for?" I asked.

Kaye turned the parchment over. "He doesn't say anything about a key in the note." He sighed. "The Day of Remembrance is only two days away. We need to get to Rombauer Castle as soon as possible. Let's leave at first light."

Beau nodded. "Then we should sleep now, while we have a fire and a roof over our heads. We won't have those if we camp along the road tomorrow night."

"Well, Reggie can always build us a fire," Kaye said. "We know how much he likes burning things." They started laughing, holding blankets to their faces so they wouldn't wake Odessa.

"That's not fair!" I said, but they kept laughing anyway. I turned over and tried to go to sleep, but something was wrong. "I hear something," I said. I walked around a screen and saw a face in the tiny window by the door. It was Birket. We stared at each other for a frozen moment while my heart thundered in my ears. I swallowed hard and said, "They found us. They followed us. I knew I heard footsteps behind us on the way here—but I didn't see anyone."

Kaye and Beau peeped around the screen. At the sight of them, Birket's droopy mouth curled into a grin, and he said something to the ground below. He disappeared and someone began banging into the front door, trying to break through. Odessa climbed down the ladder, clutching a cloak around her shoulders, her eyes wide with fright.

"Come quickly!" she said, pushing us away from the front door. "We must go out the back before they realize it's easier to get in that way. They'll have to run down the street and find an alley that lets them through. Then they'll come back this way. We have only a few moments."

We snatched up our things and followed Odessa into the alley. She turned left and then, just before we reached a big main street, she turned right, into a tiny alley behind a big building. Odessa knocked at the back door and when it opened, we stepped inside a dim room warm with the smell of baking bread.

I looked around the bakery. Two workers kneaded dough. Another shoveled loaves in and out of an enormous oven, heated by the largest fire I had ever seen. I pushed back the hood of my cloak. For the first time in ages, I felt almost too warm.

While Odessa explained our problem to her friend the baker, Kaye let himself into the front of the shop and found a small side window facing the alley. We followed him, hiding below the window.

After a while, Kaye peeped through the window lattice. "There they are," he whispered. Beau and I looked over his shoulder. Birket and Fulkes stood looking helplessly up and down the busy street. Fulkes stood on his tiptoes and jumped into the air, trying to see some sign of us. He took a feeble step into the crowds of sullen-faced men roaming the streets, but after another moment of looking, his shoulders slumped and he returned to the alley.

"They're gone," Fulkes said. "We'll never find them in the crowds now. We might as well get some sleep."

"Where will we sleep?" Birket asked. "We can't go back to the warehouse. All those angry men are there, shouting that the baron should pay them."

Fulkes snorted. "They can shout all they want. The baron won't hear them. He's at Rombauer Castle, waiting for us. Let's sleep in that house the boys just left. It's empty and there's a fire. Probably food too."

"But what will the baron say when we show up without the boys and the placards?" Birket asked, his voice quavering. "He'll kill us for sure. Remember after the boys escaped from the abbey, the baron said he'd wear our skulls for earrings if we made any more mistakes."

"The boys will be going to Rombauer Castle too," Fulkes said. "We'll catch them on the road tomorrow—or at least one of them. One will be enough." Fulkes grinned and my scalp prickled with fear. What if they caught me? I was a nobody. The baron would kill me for sure.

Fulkes and Birket ambled back up the alley toward Odessa's house and disappeared.

"We need to get on the road tonight," Kaye said as we returned to the back of the bakery.

"But we're so tired!" I said. "We've barely gotten any sleep at all lately."

"He's right, Kaye," Beau said. "We need to sleep."

Kaye scrunched up his face in thought. "I am tired," he said with a huge yawn. "But I don't know how long it takes to get to Rombauer Castle. We can't risk my father's life just to take a nap."

One of the bakers spoke up, "It takes a day and a half of walking to get to Rombauer Castle."

"But we have horses," I said, "so we'll get there even sooner."

Beau nodded. "We'll ride all day tomorrow and get there the next day long before the jousting begins. That's plenty of time to warn the king and your father."

Kaye nodded. "We'll rest here for a few hours then. But we're leaving tomorrow before sunrise. We need to get far ahead of the baron's men. We can't let them stop us from getting to the king in time."

CHAPTER fifteen

When we woke, the baker's workmen were gone, but we heard a lady's voice in the front of the shop talking to some customers.

Kaye glanced out the window at the bright sunlight. "We overslept! How could we do that? Come on, we have to get going *now!*"

Odessa came to the back of the bakery with some fresh loaves. "The baker's lady gave you these for your journey," she said.

"Have you gone home yet, Odessa?" Kaye asked.

"No, but the house is empty. Those men are gone. One of the bakers checked early this morning."

Kaye frowned. "Well, maybe it's better if they got a head start. At least they won't be following us. We just have to get to my father in time to stop the joust."

We fetched our horses and soon found the Rombauer Road, a broad and well-used road leading through a forest of ancient trees. Crowds of travelers filled the road, including many members of the baron's unpaid army. I overheard them talking and found out they were hoping to demand their money from the baron at the festival.

"Have fun with that," I muttered to myself.

"What did you say?" a man walking near me asked. He was a big man with shaggy yellow hair, reminding me of a walking straw stack. His tiny wife walked at his side. He stuck out a huge hand. "I'm Ralf," he said with a big smile.

"Oh, um, I'm Reggie. I didn't know so many people would be going to the castle," I said.

"Aye," he said. "There'll be feasting for all, and games and jousts and dancing and prizes. It will last for days! The king holds the best festivals."

"You mean the Pretender does," his wife snipped at him.

"Now, Anne, Pretender or not, King Aldric has ruled us well for many years. Why change what works?"

"Because it's not right! He's not royalty. I've seen those placards. Baron Thomas should rule Eldridge. Our own Baron Stout says the same thing."

Ralf frowned and turned back to me, changing the subject. "I like the jousting best," he said. "All the knights of Eldridge take their turn. This year, even the king himself will joust with Sir Henry, to show the rest of the knights how it's done. It will be a fine match. The king was a mighty warrior in his day, and Sir Henry is the best jouster in Eldridge since King Aethelfred himself."

I soon said good-bye to Ralf because Kaye pushed us hard that morning. We covered many miles, watching out for Fulkes and Birket, but we saw no sign of them.

We stopped for the noon meal, joining a small group of people who had cooked up a fine hot pot of stew, full of cabbage, peas, and onions, with a little bit of meat. They were happy to share their meal when we offered them some of our bread.

After eating, we listened to the other travelers sing songs and tell stories, but soon the loudest storyteller began a new tale about Sir Donkey. In this story, the king had grown tired of Sir Donkey's ridiculousness, so he sent him away on a made-up quest to another country, telling him to bring back the most beautiful thing he could find in that land. Sir Donkey vowed not to disappoint the king. He set out, crossing the border by night. However, soon after he arrived in the new country, he had the misfortune to fall headfirst into a cesspit.

The other travelers burst into laughter, and the storyteller continued. "Sir Donkey remained in the pit for four whole days—the hottest days of summer." The audience groaned in disgust. One little boy with a missing front tooth pretended to throw up.

"One evening, a shepherd heard Sir Donkey's cries and pulled him out with a rope, which smelled so bad afterward that the shepherd had to burn it. But Sir Donkey was not as grateful as he should have been."

"What happened?" someone called out.

The storyteller replied, "Sir Donkey turned to the shepherd and said, 'Good Sir, I have explored every crack and crevice of your country, and I must say, I have seen pleasanter places. I encourage you to leave, as I am doing right now. Allow me to save you from this terrible place. Come back with me to my own country, where you will find fresh air and heavenly scented flowers and wonderful perfumes. It will truly be a paradise for you.'

"The confused shepherd politely said no, and Sir Donkey returned home alone, thoroughly disgusted at the filthy country he was leaving."

Again the listeners burst into laughter at the idea of stupid Sir Donkey thinking a cesspit was an entire country, but I waited. I knew there would be more. The storyteller looked all around the group, making sure every eye was upon him, and then he said, "And oh, friends, you should have seen the gift he took to the king!"

That was the end. The people laughed so hard, some of them had to lie down flat on the forest floor until they could stop. Even I had to work hard to keep myself from smiling.

Kaye turned bright red and said, "How could anyone know about the cesspit? Only the monks and the baron knew about it. They've been spreading tales about me! We need to leave. Now."

"But we're resting!" I cried.

"There's no time to waste," Kaye said.

"Fine," I grumbled. "Just give me a moment. I need to make water." I left the group and stood behind a big tree. I couldn't believe Kaye was making us leave so soon. We'd surely be there in plenty of time to stop the joust.

As soon as I fastened my pants, I felt a sharp blow on my head from behind. "Hey!" I yelled, twisting around to see my attacker. I couldn't see his face. He wore a hood pulled over his head so low he'd had to cut out eye holes in order to see. He wrapped his arms around me and dragged me backwards. "Help!" I hollered, wondering if anyone would hear me. "HELP!"

CHAPTER SIXTEEN

The man tried to pull me deeper into the forest, but I kicked and hollered and wrapped my arms around a tree. He clamped a hand over my mouth, but I bit him really hard and kept yelling for help.

Several men from our luncheon party crashed through the trees. "Here you, let him go!" they cried.

They rushed at us and the attacker dropped me and ran. I sat up, rubbing my head. A few men kept chasing the attacker, but they lost him in the forest.

My friends rushed to my side. "What happened?" they asked.

The whole crowd wanted to know what happened. They gathered around, listening. "I was coming back to the fire when something hit my head, but it slid off to one side when it hit me," I said. The crowd nodded, waiting for the next part.

"I turned around and saw a man wearing a big hood pulled down low. He tried to drag me into the woods, but I yelled and kicked and bit him. Then all of you came and the man dropped me and ran."

Everyone murmured in astonishment and fear. They enjoyed a frightening true story with a happy ending. I had a feeling my tale would be quite famous before the day ended.

Beau and Kaye helped me back to the clearing.

"Can you keep going, Reggie?" Kaye asked.

"Yes," I said, feeling my head for a lump. "We have to."

"Then let's go," Kaye said. As we approached, our horses tossed their heads and made unhappy noises. A young woman with stringy brown hair tried to calm them by petting their necks. Placards covered the ground around the horses' feet. Someone had been digging through our saddlebags!

The woman said, "A man opened your saddlebags when everyone rushed into the forest. Me and Walter chased him off, didn't we?" She grinned at a little boy by her side.

"We threw sticks and stones at him," the boy said, giving us an adorable gap-toothed smile. It was the same boy who had pretended to throw up during the Sir Donkey tale.

"I don't think he stole anything," the woman added. "We got rid of him pretty quick."

Our noontime friends warned us to be careful. "Someone out there is after you boys," an old man said. "Don't ride by yourselves."

"We'll find a safe group to join," Beau told him.

Once we were on the road again, I told Kaye and Beau, "Fulkes attacked me, I know it. The man was too short and square to be Birket."

"I believe you," Kaye said, "but I wonder why they keep attacking you. This is the second time they've gone after you. I'm the baron's enemy, not you."

We rode onward in silence. Much later, as the sun sank low in the sky and seemed to be picking up speed as it fell toward the ground, Kaye finally said, "We have hundreds of placards in our bags, but Fulkes and Birket didn't take them. There must be something important about one of them. We need to look at them again."

"All of them?" I asked, groaning inside.

"Yes," Kaye said. "I wanted to ride a long way tonight, but if I have something that's important to the baron, I need to know what it is."

So we left the road and found a cozy spot in the forest. We let the horses graze nearby, but Kaye insisted we leave them saddled so we could keep traveling after we looked at the placards.

"Won't you make us a fire, Reggie?" Beau asked with a laugh as he dumped all the placards on the ground next to Kaye.

"Yes, you're so good at burning things," Kaye said.

I scowled, but I built a little fire. Plenty of other campers nearby had fires too, so ours didn't stand out. The horses didn't like it. They followed their noses away from the fire and around a bush, where the grass grew more thickly.

Kaye and Beau sifted through the mound of placards, carefully reading each one. I wasn't much help because I took too long to read. So I organized the heap of placards into a neat pile instead. Then I noticed something different about one of them.

"Look at this one," I said, handing it to Kaye.

He read it and raised his eyebrows. "It's an edict," he said, giving it to Beau.

"What's that?" I asked.

"It's a proclamation made by a powerful person—it's just like a law. This edict was made by the Bishop of Newksbury back when King Aethelfred was still alive. King Aethelfred also signed it and sealed it, so it shows the king approved of it."

"So the bishop made a law?" I asked. "What was it?"

"That Eldridge would remain divided into two kingdoms— Eldridge and Knox—and that they would continue to be ruled over by the sons of the dead twin princes," Beau said.

"What's new about that?" I asked.

Kaye scooted next to Beau and read over his shoulder. "It's dated just two days before King Aethelfred's death. This is one of the last things he ever did. Maybe this is the lost document that the bishop and the king made right before they died."

"The one that fell down the well with the bishop? But why would they divide the kingdom all over again? It was already done!" I said, feeling frustrated. "Dividing the kingdom is what started all the trouble!"

Beau explained, "It says in here that King Aethelfred was saddened when his people would not accept his decision to divide the kingdom. He hoped that this edict, which shows his decision is approved by the bishop and once again made into law, would help the two kingdoms live in peace alongside each other from that day forth."

I didn't know what to do with the rest of the placards, so I kept sorting them into neat piles. "Wait a minute," I said. "Is this another edict?" I picked up another parchment that didn't match the other placards and passed it to Kaye.

Kaye snatched it up and read it. "Oh," he said. "This edict says that King Aethelfred regrets his decision to divide the kingdom and that he now leaves the entire kingdom—Knox and Eldridge, together—to be ruled by his youngest son, Prince Enulf. It's also signed by the Bishop of Newksbury and dated two days before King Aethelfred's death."

"Why would he make two edicts on the same day that say two completely different things?" Beau wondered out loud.

"Maybe he changed his mind," I said.

"Maybe," Kaye said, laying the two documents side by side and studying them intently. "So why does the baron want these edicts so badly?"

"Think about it," Beau said. "Both edicts are dated the same day, and both documents look alike, except for the wording. I think one of them is real and one of them is false."

"Oh," I said. "I bet the false one is the one that says the king decided to give the whole kingdom to his youngest son. Remember Azam said the baron is related to the royal line, but only through the youngest son. The baron can use that edict to prove he should be king."

"We'll take the edicts to King Aldric," Kaye said. "Maybe he can figure out which one is real and which one is false—although I think the one about Enulf is false. It looks newer than the other one." Kaye stacked the edicts on top of each other, rolled them up, and slid them into the bag he wore at his waist.

"I'll put the placards away," I said. "We might need them later." I carried them to the horses and stuffed them back into the saddlebags. Feeling hungry, I took a loaf of bread and some oatcakes out of my own saddlebag and returned to the fire.

"It's time to eat!" I said, waving my loaf about.

One of our horses whinnied. "There's Parsnip," I said. "You know, it's funny—a few months ago, I could barely ride a horse, and now it seems like that's all I do."

"Here, give me some bread," Beau said. "I'm hungry enough to eat bark!" He grabbed a loaf out of my hand, ripped off a big chunk with his teeth, and struggled to fit the whole lump of bread in his mouth so he could chew it.

Kaye grabbed the loaf for himself and sank his own teeth into it. "Don't you know that bread must be cut, not broken, and never torn with the teeth? A knight must have the manners of a gentleman. That's one of the first things my father taught me." Kaye's face fell. "That was back when I was good at being a knight. No one cut bread more politely than me—except my father, of course."

Parsnip whinnied again, a sad sound echoing the tone of Kaye's words.

I asked something I had been wondering for a while. "Kaye, why do you think you have to be exactly like your father?"

"Because he's a perfect knight, and he was training me to be one too, ever since I was small. I used to make him so proud, but when the training got harder, I wasn't as good at it like I was with the easy things he taught me first. After a while he stopped smiling or being proud of me, and then he left me for good and came here," Kaye said, all in one breath.

"I don't understand," Beau said.

"He wants to make him proud again," I said.

Kaye nodded, but wouldn't look at us. He poked the fire with a stick.

"Of course he's proud of you, Kaye," Beau said. "You've done amazing things and you've worked a lot harder than a grown knight would have to work to do those same things. We're all proud of your hard work."

Kaye shrugged. It was like our words hit the surface of his ears but never went inside. Maybe he needed something more than words to convince him he was a good knight in his own way, even if he wasn't exactly like his father. But I didn't know what would help.

Parsnip whinnied again, sounding farther away than before. "That's strange," I said. "Parsnip almost never makes noise. I'll go check on her."

When I stepped around the bush, I only saw a few of the baron's placards littering the ground.

"Kaye! Beau!" I cried, "The horses are gone!"

CHAPTER SEVENTEEN

Beau found some men's footprints heading back to the main road. We followed the tracks, but when we reached the road, there was no sign of either the horses or the thieves.

"Oh, we should have kept them next to us!" I groaned as we returned to the clearing.

"It had to be Fulkes and Birket," Kaye said. "The baron sent them after the edicts. They probably tried searching our saddlebags for them, but it was too dark and the horses were too noisy for them to risk staying. So they took the saddlebags and the horses."

He sat down in the dirt with a thump and buried his face in his hands. "How could I be so stupid? Everyone knows you keep your horses in plain sight when there are wicked men about. Oh, what would my father do?" he murmured into his palms.

"He'd keep going," Beau said. "And it's exactly what you're going to do."

"It's what you always do, Kaye," I said.

Our little fire cast a dim light on Kaye, but through the patchy shadows across his face, he regarded us steadily. Then he stood up. "You're right," he said. "We have to keep going. If our horses are gone, then we'll walk, even if we have to walk all night. I have to save my father and the king."

There was no point in resting anymore. We had no idea how long it would take us to reach the castle now that we were on foot. Beau put out the fire and I packed our leftover food into my provision bag.

"At least we still have the edicts," Kaye whispered. "Let's go."

I'll always remember that night. I have never walked so long or so hard or so fast. Kaye spurred us on. "We have to go faster," he kept saying. "We'll never make it in time."

Only toward dawn did he let us sit down. We drank from a chilly spring and dipped our tired feet into it. Kaye let us rest only as long as it took to put on our stockings and boots again. Then he drove us onward.

My eyelids drooped and my head kept nodding, and then I'd stumble over my own feet as I drifted off. Once in a while, I noticed Kaye and Beau doing the same thing, but my eyes were closed more than they were open.

"Is it possible to sleep and walk at the same time?" I wondered.

"Yes. It's called sleepwalking," Beau said.

"That's not what I meant!" I said, too tired to argue about it any further. "I keep almost falling."

"Just pick up your feet and put them down again, one after the other," Kaye encouraged me.

"Thank you so much, Kaye, for the excellent walking instructions," I muttered to myself.

"What did you say?" he asked as he lurched along beside me.

I sighed. "I already know how to walk. I just don't know how to *keep* walking," I explained.

"It's the same thing," he said. "Just one foot after another until we find the king and my father."

Around sunrise, other people appeared on the road again, all of them eager to reach the castle.

"It's not far now, Mary," a man said to his wife.

"That's good, dear," she said.

"Really?" I asked, opening my eyes fully for the first time since we began our midnight trek.

"Truly," he said with an annoyingly cheerful smile. "Only a few more hours of walking and we'll be at the castle in time for the noonday feast."

A few more hours! I tried very hard to smile back at that cheerful man, but it took so much strength to curl my lips upwards, that I gave up halfway through and closed my eyes again.

"Mary, get away from that boy," the man said. "There's something wrong with him. He may be dangerous." They hurried away.

Kaye snorted with laughter. "You looked ridiculous." He made his neck fall forward and his head fall backward, shutting his eyes halfway and pulling the edges of his open mouth upwards in an expression that was both pained and idiotic-looking. "That's how you looked," he said.

"No wonder your horse ran away from you," Beau said, laughing like a loon.

"She didn't run away, she was stolen!" I said in indignation.

"She probably begged the thief to take her," Kaye said.

"Ha, ha," I said. "Very funny. Now leave me alone, I'm trying to sleep." I clamped my eyes shut and plodded onward, peering through the cracks in my eyelids every now and then to make sure I wasn't about to walk into a tree.

Kaye walked behind me, steering me by the shoulders, propelling me forward faster and faster. "What are you doing?" I asked. "Why are we going so fast?"

"The man said we'd get there in time for the noon meal, but Azam's letter said the exhibition joust between my father and the king is right before the noon feast. We have to go faster. We're running out of time," Kaye puffed over my shoulder, growing short of breath.

I worried about him. Fear for his father's life was eating him up like a broken-toothed worm gnawing its way through his insides. So I kept quiet, and let Kaye shove me awkwardly along the road like a wagon in front of a horse.

Beau followed in our wake, murmuring encouragement, although it didn't work very well—I could only hear one word in every ten.

"Keep on... good... walking... more... little farther... one foot... good... foot... more...just..." He trailed into silence and then tripped over his boots. With a stumbling dance, he barely saved himself from falling, making some children nearby almost break into pieces with laughter.

"Just keep going," Kaye said, his voice dry and raspy. I twisted around to look at him. His eyes burned with alertness, his head twitching with a startled jerk toward every new noise he heard.

By the third hour, the forest thinned and the road broadened and broke free of the trees. The harvested fields surrounding us looked freshly shaved, now that they were stripped of their gleaming stalks of barley and wheat.

About an hour later, we crested a hill and finally saw the large city of Rombauer below us, and at the far side of it, Rombauer Castle, where the tournament was being held. We heard distant trumpets and then cheers.

Kaye turned a stricken face to us. "The jousting has already started," he said. "We're too late!"

chapter eighteen

"It's all right, Kaye," Beau said. "There's a lot of jousting that has to happen in a tournament. The king's joust is right before the noon meal. That gives us two hours to get across this city and to the jousting field. I think we can do it."

We could have traveled that distance in one hour if there hadn't been so many other people on the road. Everyone going to the castle seemed excited to get there, but as a group, they walked more slowly than a bear waking up from his winter's sleep, blinking and staring at everything new that came along.

I couldn't blame them. Even I began to wake up, seeing all the sights of this fine, large city dressed up for a celebration. I gasped at the sight of the enormous wall surrounding the city, taller than a tree and built of stones like golden sand. Kingsbridge had been a big city, but it was sloppy and disorganized, full of constant comings and goings with the sea so close at hand. Rombauer City was neat and orderly, a city built to do a king credit, and it had all its best clothes on that day. Ropes of flowers hung across the road, draped from window to window of the houses lining each side of the street. The houses were built with their largest rooms on top, sticking out over the road and overshadowing it, so it felt like we were traveling through a long cave with a roof made of flowers.

Vendors called out that they had fried dough, pickled beets, or dried figs for sale. One man roasted meat on a spit, sending a rich, crackling aroma into the air, waking me up even more by reminding me how hungry I was.

I found a coin in my pocket, and the man sold me a penny-worth of meat, carving it off the side of his roast, the brown juices flowing. I opened a piece of our bread from the night before to catch the meat as it fell off the roast beneath his knife. It was hot! Too hot to hold. I clapped the bread around the meat so I wouldn't burn my fingers.

I had to run to catch up with the others. Kaye looked at me, a vein pulsing in his temple, and said in a weary voice, "Reggie. We don't have time to stop for anything."

"I caught up with you again," I said. "And we haven't eaten for hours. Look!" I held out my meat inside its blanket of bread. "Have some. We need food. We can eat and walk, even if we can't sleep and walk."

"Speak for yourself," Beau mumbled, scuffing his feet along the road, his eyes barely open.

Kaye waved the food away, so I offered it to Beau. He took a little bite, opened his eyes all the way, and took another, bigger bite. After a few more bites, he seemed like a new man. I had a few bites myself. The bread cradled the hot, juicy meat, soaking up all the goodness. Four bites of that meat and bread was almost as good as an hour's sleep. Almost.

"Kaye, you need food," I said. "Take the rest; it's yours."

Kaye barely shook his head no. He fixed his eyes on the outline of the castle towers looming over the edge of the city like a protective guardian.

Exasperated with Kaye's fixation, I tried bribing him. "Kaye, if you eat this, Beau and I will run the rest of the way to the castle with you."

Kaye didn't respond. Beau shrugged. I tried once more. "Kaye, your father would eat it. He would know that he needed energy for whatever lies ahead."

Kaye tore his gaze from the towers and looked at me. His eyes fell to the food I held out to him. He took a deep breath, swallowed, and nodded.

As soon as he took the food, his eyes snapped back to the towers and he ate mechanically, walking even faster, as if to make up for the time lost chewing, not even noticing the genius of my bread-as-a-hot-meat-holder idea.

When the last morsel of food had disappeared, he said, "Now we run."

"What?" I said. "I only said that so you would eat the food."

"I ate the food," Kaye said.

"No, you ate the food because I said your father would. That was a different reason. Not because I promised to run. You ignored that idea. Besides, look at this crowd. They're blocking us and they walk slower than oxen."

"Hey!" the man next to me said. "Watch who you call an ox."

"Sorry," I muttered.

Kaye looked at us, his eyes large and sticking out much more than usual. "We have to run. Look at the sky. It's almost noon. If we don't, we'll be too late."

Without another word, he ran, piercing the crowds like a needle through cloth. Beau and I did the same, much more clumsily, bumping into people's elbows and bouncing off their arms as we tried to follow his threadlike path through the masses of travelers and festival-goers.

The crowd soon separated us and I was alone. I panicked, remembering the feel of Fulkes grabbing hold of me with arms like bands of iron. Then I panicked at being lost, not knowing how I would ever find Kaye and Beau again.

But then I realized we were all going to the same place. We were the only three people in the whole city who knew what was about to happen and wanted to stop it. Whichever of us reached the king first had to stop the assassination.

So I pushed onward, stepping on toes and crashing into people, ignoring their cries of outrage and pain. I felt like a mole, blindly digging a tunnel through that mass of people, only knowing that I had to keep tunneling toward the castle or everything would be lost. If one of us didn't get there in time, all these crowds of festive merry-makers would suddenly be weeping for their king.

I pushed harder. Waves of indignation rippled through the crowd around me. A man grabbed my shoulder, saying, "I'll teach you some manners, whelp!"

I jumped, thinking that Fulkes or Birket had gotten hold of me, but when I realized it was just an ordinary man, I wormed away from him and soon reached the castle gates.

A solid block of people pressed through the gates, but I spotted a tiny crack in the crowd, dove through it, and ran toward the castle, gulping in air like I hadn't breathed in a month. I tried to ignore the pounding in my chest and the waves of heat washing over my head as I looked around. Everyone turned to the right once they were inside the castle walls. I ran that way too and soon found myself in the thick of the tournament spectators.

We had arrived just in time! A man on a raised platform shouted out that the king would now give a jousting demonstration with Eldridge's Friend, the illustrious Sir Henry. The crowd burst into a roar of approval for the king and Sir Henry. Surely

Kaye would be proud to see how much the Eldridge people loved Sir Henry. I hoped Kaye was here. If not, I had to stop the joust, but I couldn't see anything—only the shoulders and backs of the people in front of me.

I shoved through the crowd until I reached the fence marking the edge of the lists—the open space where the king and Sir Henry at this very moment leveled their lances and began galloping toward each other. My heart held its breath. I had to stop them!

Just then, Kaye and Beau burst through the edge of the crowd and leapt over the fence. "Here you, stop that!" called a castle guard.

"Catch that boy, he can't be there!" another one said, grabbing hold of Beau and stopping him from following Kaye.

A third one ran onto the field, chasing after Kaye, but Kaye feinted to the right, dodged to the left, and eluded his grasp.

The horses' galloping hooves must have drowned out the noise the guards and Kaye were making, because the king and Sir Henry kept pounding steadily toward each other—and toward their own deaths.

Then Kaye tripped and fell, sprawled out on the green turf of the lists, and the guard pounced on him. The crowd laughed as Kaye fought and kicked, trying to get away, but I dashed onto the field as fast as a rabbit released from a trap. I couldn't stay to see if Kaye would get free. I had to stop the joust!

If the king was drugged with poppy syrup, like Azam had said, my best chance was to get Sir Henry's attention, so I ran toward him, flapping my cloak around like the wings of a frightened bat, trying to catch his eye. And I yelled for all I was worth, screaming, "Stop! Stop! Stop!"

It worked! Sir Henry saw me and checked his horse's pace. The king's horse kept moving toward us, but at a gentle trot now.

"Stop the joust!" I cried out. "Stop the joust! The king will die!"

I pointed at Sir Henry's lance, but he shook his head in confusion. In desperation, I grabbed his lance and dashed its false tip against the ground. The crowd gasped as I held it up, revealing its wicked metal point.

Sir Henry seized the lance and inspected it, twisting around in his saddle to look for the man who had handed it to him. Of course that man was long gone. Then he looked at me. "Reggie?" he asked in surprise. Then he looked behind me. "Kaye? What are you doing here?"

The king's horse was upon us! I leapt out of the way and the king's lance crashed into the armor covering Sir Henry's chest. The gaudy blue and gold lance shattered into as many splinters as there are stars in the sky, and the king himself rolled gently backward off his horse and hit the ground in a clatter of armor.

In the moment of horrified silence that followed, the king's horse walked back to him and sniffed the metal-plated body lying in a heap on the soft green grass.

I glanced at Sir Henry, who was gazing at himself in wonder that he was unharmed. Somebody had to see if the king was still alive. I ran to him, dropping to my knees next to his body. I heard him inhale and exhale.

"He breathes!" I cried out.

As if that were the sign to bring everyone back to life, the spectators roared out cheers of joy and exclamations of dismay and horror. I touched the king's hand. It felt cold. Why didn't he move?

CHAPTER NINETEEN

Excited chatter erupted throughout the crowd like water bursting through a dam. Guards ran out onto the field. Sir Henry dismounted and knelt next to me and the king. He gently removed the king's helmet.

"Praise be," Sir Henry said, "his neck is not broken."

"Shurtainly not," the king murmured, lifting his head slightly and opening his eyelids a crack. Sir Henry slipped a hand under the king's head to support it. "Shurtainly not broken. What a dishgrace that would be." He fell asleep again and his head plopped back down. Sir Henry lowered it softly to the grass.

"He's drugged with poppy juice," I said.

"How on earth did you know about this?" Sir Henry asked.

"Baron Thomas is behind this," I said. "He wanted to frame you for killing the king so he could kill you in vengeance, take the throne for himself, declare war on Knox, conquer it, and rule over Eldridge and Knox together as one country. Kaye found out the plot."

Guards approached and lifted the king, carrying him off the field. Kaye and Beau appeared behind Sir Henry's shoulder. Sir Henry looked up and saw them. "Hello, Your Grace," he said to Beau. Then he wrapped his arm around Kaye. "My boy," he said. "I was never so surprised to see anyone in my life." Sir Henry rested his other hand on my shoulder and added, "Your friend Reggie is as brave and courageous as the best knights in

Knox. He saved the king and the peace. You should be proud of him. I know I am."

I froze, every muscle paralyzed. Sir Henry's words seemed to swirl in the air and drift slowly downward over us, like fat snowflakes falling on a silent graveyard. His words made me happy, but I dreaded meeting Kaye's eyes. Sir Henry should have been saying those words to him. They were what Kaye had been waiting to hear, what Kaye had been working for all this time.

Kaye refused to look at me. Instead, he threw his arms around Sir Henry, burying his face in his father's neck, saying, "Oh, Father, I'm so glad you're alive."

"Me too," Sir Henry said, rising to his feet. "So Baron Thomas really thought that if he framed me for killing the king that the people of Eldridge would accept him with open arms as the new king?"

"That wasn't his first plot, sir," Beau said. "His first plot was to hire a whole army to attack the king's castle and take the throne by force. Kaye ruined that for him, so this is his second plan."

"How did you stop him from hiring an army?" Sir Henry asked Kaye.

Kaye's pointed face lit up with his triangular smile. "I took his gems so he couldn't pay his army!" he said with glee. "They were balas rubies. I hid them. I'll tell you all about the legend of the forest beast and how we used it to scare the baron's guards away long enough for us to hide the rubies."

"I want to hear all about it," Sir Henry said. "And I want to know more about this Sir Donkey business."

Kaye's face fell. "Oh, no. I was hoping you hadn't heard about that."

Sir Henry smiled. "You know what they say. Good news travels fast, but bad news travels faster. But I also know there's more to every story than you hear. I want to know the whole story."

With a sigh, Kaye said, "I'll tell you, but I hate that story."

"Let's go to the castle and look in on the king first. Then I want to know why you're here and how you got here. I know you all came to stop me from killing the king, which Reggie did so well, but surely there's more to that story."

Kaye finally looked at me. And when he did, I wished he hadn't. His eyes were not the warm eyes of a friend, and what's worse, he looked disgusted, like he had just stepped on a slimy slug in his bare feet—like the sight of me made him want to throw up.

"I'm so sorry, Kaye," I whispered, "I know you wanted to save your father yourself. But you couldn't get there in time. So I did it. There was no time to wait."

Kaye curled his lip like he had seen a repulsive centipede wriggling in his porridge. Then he turned away and ran to catch up with his father.

I sat down hard in the middle of the field. Who would have thought that saving two lives could make me feel so terrible? There had to be some way I could make it up to Kaye so we could be friends again.

Eventually I stood up. I figured I might as well go to the castle and see how King Aldric fared. After all, he was the one who suggested that the queen give me the job of Royal Chronicler. So we had been friends of a sort, once upon a time. Of course, I had been friends with Kaye once upon a time too, and now I knew how quickly that could change.

I found my way to the great hall of the castle and peeped inside. It was full of feasting, merry-making, and dancing—the dancers wore costumes and masks, in colors as bright as stained glass windows! A long line of dancers skipped forward, hands held high. I gasped when I saw that at least four of the men wore different sorts of costumes to make them look like donkeys. Sir Donkey was alive and well at this masked ball, and Kaye would be miserable over it.

I stepped a little farther into the great hall to see if Kaye was there, but the guard just inside the door noticed me and gestured to some trumpeters lounging against the wall. They stood up straight, lifted their long, thin trumpets into an even line, and blew a fanfare.

The music stopped and the dancers froze, dropping their hands to their sides. The feasters even stopped in mid-chew. Into this silence, the guard shouted, "Behold the savior of our king, Master Reggie Stork!"

I blushed as everyone shouted, "Huzzah! Huzzah!"

People had cheered for me before, and I had enjoyed it, but this time it felt empty. My gaze floated to the top of the room, where Kaye, Beau, and Sir Henry sat at the king's table. I met Kaye's hurt eyes, and I knew why. When Sir Henry set a seat for me between him and Kaye, I felt like my guts were made of lead. I plopped down in my chair like a bagful of rocks.

This was a king's feast on a special feast day. Every food I could imagine passed in front of me—roast swan, roast peacock, roast boar, but even though I hadn't eaten for hours and had walked all night, I had no heart to taste any of the astounding food before me. I put a few things on my trencher and looked at them. I couldn't bear to eat. I had to try again. I turned to my friend. "Kaye, I'm so sorry, I didn't mean to take your place."

Kaye stared at the costumed dancers in front of him, his own plate full of untouched food. His tired eyes looked dried up and far away. He tried swallowing, but needed to sip his drink before he could manage it. Finally he licked his lips and whispered, "Thank you for saving their lives. That was the most important thing. I couldn't do it. I could only fall flat on my face like Sir Donkey always does."

"Kaye," I said.

Kaye held up his hand to stop me. He still wouldn't look at me. He shook his head, folding his lips into a tight smile as he gestured to the four Sir Donkey costumes that now pranced together around the floor in a circle as people laughed and clapped and pointed. "Look. I'm a famous knight. People sing songs and tell stories about me. That's all I ever wanted, and I got it, but for all the wrong reasons. I wanted to be famous for being a *good* knight, like my father," he said.

"Kaye," I said, but again he stopped me.

"I'm sorry, Reggie," he said, standing up and pushing in his chair. "I'm very glad you saved their lives, but right now I have a hard time even looking at you. It hurts my stomach. When I heard my father saying all those things about you..." He trailed off and stared at the back of the chair for a moment. "It was supposed to be *me*," he said to the chair. Kaye turned and left the room through a side door.

Stunned by his last words, I stared after him. What had just happened?

CHAPTER TWENTY

After a moment, Sir Henry noticed Kaye's empty seat. "Where's Kaye?" he asked. "Gone to use the privy?"

I shook my head. "He's upset."

Sir Henry frowned for a moment. "Well, he told me you boys walked all night. Perhaps he needs to rest. He'll be just fine in the morning."

I shook my head again. "No, sir, I think he needs you."

"Me? What for?" Sir Henry said.

"Maybe you should go find out," I said.

Sir Henry wiped his mouth carefully before sipping his drink and saying, "I will. But you should come too. You can help me find him."

"He doesn't want to see me right now," I said.

"Nonsense," Sir Henry said. "You're his best friend. I remember how happy he was to introduce me to you last time I was in Knox. Why wouldn't he want to see you?"

It was too hard to explain. I stood up, glancing at my trencher. Three palm-sized meat pies and a large chunk of apple tart sat there, waiting to be eaten. I hated to waste them. I gathered them up, tucked them in my bag, and followed Sir Henry out the side door of the great hall.

He glanced back at me as I pinned my cloak around my shoulders. "Do you always prepare for a long journey when you leave dinner?" he asked.

I smiled a little, but it hurt. "No, but it's always good to carry food. And I brought the cloak because it's cold out, and with Kaye, you never know what will happen. He gets us into all kinds of adventures, but he always finds a way out. He's very determined."

Sir Henry chuckled. "He always was, even as a little boy. I remember when I began training him. He would never quit trying something until he learned how to do it, even if he turned himself black and blue in the meantime."

"Hmph," I said. Kaye was still turning himself black and blue, but now it was on the inside. Since Kaye was already mad at me, I decided to tell Sir Henry something that would make Kaye even madder if he ever found out.

"Kaye thinks you left Knox because he wasn't doing well with his training and you were disappointed in him. He's afraid you thought he wouldn't ever become a good knight. That's why he tries so hard to be a knight just like you and why he's so upset about being Sir Donkey."

Sir Henry turned to stare at me. In the dim torchlight of the stone hallway, I could see a little tremor in his hand as he held it up. "Kaye thinks I left because I thought he was a failure? All this time he's been thinking that?"

I nodded. "He really wanted to save you today, but he fell. I had to do it for him. And then you said how proud you were of me and how I was as good as the best knights in Knox. That hurt him. He wanted to hear you say those things about him."

"But I'm *so* proud of him," Sir Henry said, putting his hand to his brow. "He's done everything I ever wanted to do for him—all by himself. He became a knight, helps the queen, and keeps up with his training..." His voice trailed off. "And he's a good boy—noble, courageous, loyal—everything I ever wanted him to be." Sir Henry looked at me. "I need to tell him that."

"Yes," I said, but my voice gave away my doubts.

"What is it?" Sir Henry asked.

"Beau and I, we've told him all that. Many times. But it seems like he can't even hear the words anymore. He needs something more than words."

"What does he need?" Sir Henry asked.

I shrugged. "If I knew, I would have done it already." It was true. Even now that Kaye found me too disgusting to look at, I would still try to help him feel better if I knew how.

Sir Henry folded his arms in thought. "I have an idea. You say he wants to be just like me. Well, tomorrow morning I have a meeting with an ambassador from the south countries. I've been planning it for months! It will be an important step in creating a peaceful relationship with those countries and it will open up new trade routes for…"

Sir Henry kept talking as we walked, his voice bouncing with excitement about his goals for becoming friends with the south countries. I forgot to pay attention as I worried that Kaye would hate me forever. A sudden silence made me look up. Sir Henry was waiting for me to answer him.

I hung my head. "I'm sorry," I said. "I wasn't listening. I was thinking about Kaye."

"So was I," Sir Henry said. "That's why I'm inviting him to my meeting with the ambassador tomorrow morning. It will show Kaye that I take him seriously as a knight and that I want to include him in the important knightly things I do."

I frowned. "I'm not sure that's what he thinks being a knight is all about."

"Well, it's all I ever do anymore," Sir Henry said. "I think he'll be happy when I invite him. We just have to find him first. Where do you think he might be?"

"Sometimes, at Castle Forte, he goes up on the high towers at night to think. He likes to see the stars. He looks for pictures in them."

Sir Henry smiled. "I remember. We used to do that together. Come along then, let's go look for him on the towers."

Sir Henry took off down the halls, his long strides covering the distance much faster than my stubby legs. He turned a corner and I lost him, but I didn't worry because I knew I should stay away from Kaye right now. Sir Henry would take care of Kaye.

When I tried to find my way back to the great hall, I couldn't remember if we had turned left or right into this hallway. In fact, I couldn't remember which way was left and which way was right.

I slumped against a wall, pressing the side of my face into it, trying to gather enough energy to keep walking. Ordinarily, I would have loved to explore a new castle, but after walking all night, my legs and feet ached and burned. All I wanted was to close my eyes. I wondered how uncomfortable it would be to sleep here on the stone floor.

But that seemed foolish when a fine castle bed waited for me if I could just find the great hall again. There would be servants there who could show me the way to a bedchamber. I closed my eyelids to rest them.

The stone wall under my cheek grew warm, but the other cheek felt chilly. A small breeze blew on it. I opened my eyes and walked toward that breeze. I didn't know where I was going, but at least I had a guide—a tiny, invisible guide, but it seemed more reliable than my sense of direction.

Finally that chilly little finger of wind brought me to a small door propped open to the night air. I stepped through it and found myself in the main courtyard. This was perfect! I could easily find my way back to the great hall from the main entrance of the castle.

I took two steps forward only to be stopped from behind by a pair of arms that held me much too tight, wrapping around me like one of those choking snakes that press the air out of your body and crush your bones to jelly at the same time.

"Let me *go*!" I said, squirming for all I was worth. "Stop squeezing me!" I said. "It hurts!"

A raspy voice chuckled in my ear. "Oh, no. I'm not letting you get away again."

It was Fulkes. He smashed his hand over my mouth and nose. I couldn't breathe. I struggled, but my aching muscles wouldn't work. I collapsed against my captor. A red haze covered my sight. Through it I saw the moon, floating like a glowing pink bubble in the sky. I was running out of air! With my last bit of strength, I chomped down hard on the hand covering my mouth and after that, I knew no more.

chapter twenty-one

I woke up in a round, windy room made of stone. I stepped over to a small window, stuck my head out, and discovered I was in the tower of a castle on a mountain. All of Rombauer City spread out below me.

Rombauer Castle looked like a child's toy—tiny and perfect. Colored flags whipped in the breeze and a broad blue river sparkled in the sunlight as it crept along its steady course. Beside the castle, jousting knights on their horses looked like brightly-painted ants as they hurtled toward each other.

At the base of my tower, grass grew rankly in a courtyard bordering the cliff's edge. To my surprise, I saw our three stolen horses grazing among the weeds below my tower.

Beyond the quiet courtyard, groups of people moved up and down the winding road between Rombauer Castle and this ancient fortress. This must have been King Aethelfred's original castle, and the people must have been visiting because of the Day of Remembrance, but they all flocked together, far from my tower. No one would hear me if I yelled.

A gust of wind hit the tower and it swayed backward slightly. I yelped and ducked back inside the room and flung myself against the ancient-looking door. It was locked, of course, and as solid as a slab of rock.

I thought about flapping my cloak out the window. Maybe someone at the tournament would see it and come rescue me.

Maybe Kaye would—

No. Kaye couldn't stand the sight of me. He certainly wouldn't be looking for me. He probably didn't even know I was missing.

The tower groaned as the wind buffeted it again. The door to my room rattled open, and I pressed myself against the wall as Fulkes entered the room.

He grinned, showing me stained and broken teeth in his square face. "You sleep hard, boy. I carried you up the mountain and up all them stairs and dropped you here on the floor and you never woke until now." He laughed out loud, hitting me with a blast of putrid air from across the room. I wrinkled my nose.

"What do you want with me?" I asked.

He shrugged. "It's the baron who wants you. He's waiting downstairs."

Fulkes led me down hundreds of stairs and into a large room. I could see blue sky and clouds through gaps in the roof. The stones of the walls looked powdery with age. A long line of small windows near the roof let in light and air and also birds, if the white splotches on the floor told the truth. Mounds of dry leaves filled the corners of the room and the insides of two large fireplaces. A bird's nest rested on one of the mantelpieces.

A sword hung in a place of honor on the farthest wall. It looked like it had been used frequently and for many years. No gems or carvings decorated the hilt. It was a plain, strong sword, well-sharpened and dangerous.

"What's this place?" I asked.

"It's Aethelfred's old throne room," Fulkes answered in his raspy voice. "It belongs to the baron now." Fulkes stepped aside, and at the far end of the room, I saw a man sitting on a barrel in the center of a raised platform. With his trailing red cloak, droopy moustache, and long, hanging-down hair, he looked startlingly familiar. "King Aethelfred?" I whispered in wonder. "How? He's *dead!*"

After a moment, I realized the man was only dressed like King Aethelfred. Unlike King Aethelfred's long, pale face and sad, droopy eyes, this man's rosy, shiny cheeks bulged above a winged moustache in a round, red face. Instead of King Aethelfred's long, lean body, this man looked as well-muscled as a cat—and a well-fed cat at that.

The man's red-shot eyes glared at me from under a heavy gold crown set with three enormous rubies. Fulkes shoved me across the room until I stood in front him. The man looked me up and down, sniffed, and said, "I am Baron Thomas of Eldridge, soon to be king of Eldridge."

My eyes snapped up to meet his. "But Aldric is king," I said without thinking.

The baron leaped to his feet, grabbed my shoulders in his ham-like fists, and lifted me off the ground. The tip of his tilted nose turned the color of raw meat. Tiny dark-purple lines crisscrossed it like a tangle of branches caught in a stream. "It is my *right* to be king. Aldric is an imposter! He has none of Aethelfred's blood in him!"

"Do you?" I asked.

To my surprise, he calmed down, releasing his grip on my shoulders and dumping me to the floor like a heap of old clothes. He sat down on the barrel, his red cloak forming a crumpled mound behind him. "Of course I do. I'm descended from his youngest son, Enulf. Aethelfred's throne should be mine."

I stood up and pointed to the barrel where he sat. "Surely *that's* not Aethelfred's throne."

Fulkes swatted the back of my head. "Treat the baron with respect," he said, blasting me from behind with his terrible breath. I coughed.

The baron smiled broadly. "No, but I have the privilege of looking after Aethelfred's beautiful original throne. It's in my warehouse in Kingsbridge so I won't be tempted to use it here."

"Why not?"

"I made a vow," he said. "I will not use Aethelfred's throne until I have reunited Eldridge and Knox into one kingdom, the way they were when Aethelfred ruled in wisdom and strength. *Then* I will sit here, in Aethelfred's throne room, upon his throne, and I will rule this kingdom as I was meant to."

His eyes narrowed until he looked like an angry boar. He folded his arms across his chest. "But first I need that edict you and your friend stole. I need it to prove that Aethelfred left the kingdom to his youngest son Enulf and that it belongs to me now. So give it to me or I'll kill you."

I gulped at his sudden change in tone and my heart turned into a cold blob like the yolk of a raw egg. Suddenly I realized the baron had only mentioned one edict. He didn't know there were two.

Then I got annoyed. I crossed my arms and glared at him. "How can I give it to you? You didn't *warn* me that I was going to be kidnapped and to please have any important documents with me at the time."

Fulkes swatted the back of my head again, but thankfully he kept his breath to himself. The baron glared at me, hatred billowing across his face like a cloud of ink dumped in water. "Why aren't you crying and begging for your life?" he asked. "I just threatened to kill you."

Fear quivered through my bones and I swallowed hard. "Well," I said, "You won't kill me before you get your edict." I ducked before Fulkes could swat me this time.

The baron laughed through his frown. "So how will you get it for me?" he asked. "I'm not a patient man, and now that the king knows I tried to kill him, I need to leave the country immediately—especially since the other barons abandoned me when they realized I planned to murder the king. But I won't leave without that edict."

"Kaye has it," I said. "He might bring it if I asked him to." Or he might not—but I didn't tell the baron that part.

"So write to him," the baron said. "Fulkes will bring you pen and parchment and ink."

"Oh, Baron Thomas," I said, feeling suddenly more afraid than when he threatened to kill me. "I don't write so well. Wouldn't you rather write it yourself?"

"No," he said. "If you want to live, you'll write it. Tell him to bring the edict here by the sixth bell or I'll hurl you off the tower." He leered down at me. "You deserve to die. After all, *you* ruined my plan to assassinate the king"

I felt my eyes widen and struggled to shrink them back down before he noticed. "I didn't *mean* to," I said. "Well, I did mean to stop it, but the truth is that Kaye was going to do it, but he tripped and fell so I stopped it instead."

The baron began to chuckle. "That's true. He's too funny to be a knight. He ought to be a fool instead." He pursed his lips in thought. "See here, tell your Sir Donkey to come dressed like a jester, so all the world can see him for the fool he is. If he does that, I'll let you both go. Oh, and he mustn't tell anyone he's coming here."

"You want him to dress like a jester?" I said, feeling horrified. "Like in a hat with bells on it? Kaye will never do that!"

"If he wants you to live, he will. And he *will* want you to live. He's such a good little knight, always sacrificing himself to help others. Why do you think I sent my men after you instead of him? Now that I have you, I can make him do anything I want. You are my key for ruining that stupid little knight."

The baron rose from his barrel and swept out of the room with Fulkes close behind him, leaving me standing there with my mouth hanging open. The baron didn't know that the very sight of me made Kaye sick inside. He couldn't use me to make Kaye do anything now, and as soon as he realized that, I was as good as dead.

chapter twenty-two

I wrapped my arms around my middle and wondered what it would be like to die. Soon Fulkes returned, carrying a wooden tray that held a pot of ink, a pen, a parchment, some brown bread, and several lumps of pale cheese. Streaks of mold ran through the cheese like the blue-green veins under the soft side of my arm.

Fulkes set the pot of ink, pen, and parchment on the edge of the platform and pointed at me. "Write the letter now."

I took a step backward. "I'm terrible at writing," I said.

Fulkes shrugged. "Write it or die," he said.

My throat tightened as if the baron's giant hand was already wrapped around it. This was the worst situation I could imagine. I was in mortal danger, and *writing* was supposed to save my life? I sat down on the platform and fought against the panic rising like floodwaters from my gut to my throat.

I lifted the pen. Fulkes stood there, looking at me expectantly. "You should sit," I said. "I told you I'm bad at writing. This is going to take a while."

He plopped down on the edge of the platform next to me and began eating the food on his tray. He caught me looking at him. "Bite?" he offered, holding out a half-eaten hunk of bread smeared with cheese. I saw his teeth marks in the bread.

I sniffed at it and the hair on my scalp lifted straight up. The cheese smelled like a pile of unwashed stockings and all the dirty feet that ever wore them, but I hadn't eaten for fifteen hours, and my stomach rumbled loudly, demanding the food. And anything was better than writing. I held my breath and took a bite.

It was surprisingly good, but after I swallowed, my mouth tasted like something had died in it. I shot Fulkes a dirty look and hoped he'd get close enough for me to breathe on him.

Pinching my lips together hard, I wrote "Kaye—the baron took me. I am in the old castle throne room. Bring the edict by the sixth bell or he will kill me."

"Why are you so slow?" Fulkes complained. He picked up small chunks of cheese and threw them at me. They left dark splats and a strong smell on my clothes and skin. "Just write it," he said. "Write it now. I don't have all day."

I dipped my quill in the ink again and wrote, "He says to come dressed like a jester or he will kill us both. Tell no one."

I paused for a moment after dodging a lump of flying cheese. I wasn't sure Kaye would even want to come for me. If the sight of me truly made him sick, he might just stay away completely. So I wrote one more thing. "Kadar is here." If Kaye wouldn't come for me, maybe he'd come for his horse.

I had to tell Kaye that the baron only knew about one of the edicts. But how? The baron would surely read my letter.

Another pellet of cheese bounced off my cheek. "Stop staring and write!" Fulkes hollered into my ear. His breath smelled so much worse than the cheese.

Wait a moment! Maybe I *could* tell Kaye about the one edict. A slow grin spread across my face, like honey across a piece of hot bread. My writing was so bad that no one could read it except Kaye. Even Beau could only decipher a word or two of it.

I took a deep breath and wrote, "The baron thinks there is only one edict. He wants the one about Enulf. He doesn't know about the other one. Maybe you can surprise him."

I wrote my name and handed the letter to Fulkes. "I finished," I said, exhaling extra hard, so he could smell what his terrible cheese had done to my breath.

He wrinkled his nose. "Finally," he huffed. "You're the slowest writer I ever saw."

"It's true," I said. "And I'll probably always be that way." I felt a smile grow on my face all by itself.

He narrowed his eyes. "What are you so happy about?"

I shrugged. "I guess I'm proud I did it. Writing is hard for me." Then I crossed my arms and glared at him. "And being pelted with cheese doesn't help."

"I was bored," he muttered. When he leaned across me to pick up the ink bottle, I managed to breathe my stinky cheese breath all over his face one last time.

After he left, I realized I was tired of dreading the idea of writing down my Royal Chronicles. I promised myself that if I ever got back to Knox, I would start writing my book—even if it took me the rest of my life to finish it. I might never be proud of how my writing looked, but I could be proud of myself if I stuck to it.

Moments later, the baron stormed into the throne room. "What is this? A joke? I can't read a word of this!" he screamed.

"It's how I write," I said. "No one can read it except Kaye. I told you I was bad at it. I begged you to write it yourself."

He looked at me strangely. "That's true," he said. "Then you read it to me."

I read him all the parts that weren't about the two edicts. He chuckled when I read about Kaye dressing as a jester. When I finished, I held out the letter. "Do you want to rewrite this?" I asked, hoping he would be too lazy to do that.

Snatching it from my hand, he wheeled around and ambled out the door. "No," he called over his shoulder. "If no one can read this, it means that no one else will know you're here. I'd prefer *not* to have that blasted Sir Henry getting in the way." The door slammed shut and I was alone again.

I hoped Kaye would come for me.

I sat on the edge of the platform and thought I would cheer myself up by eating the meat pies in my bag, but they were gone. Fulkes must have stolen them. I threw the bag away from me, rested my chin in my hand, and prepared to listen to my stomach growl when my eye fell on a tiny, almost invisible metal circle on the floor.

"Someone dropped their ring," I thought, but when I tried to pick it up, one side of it held fast to the floor. "It must be a trapdoor," I said, tugging on it with all my might. Nothing happened. I might as well have been pulling on a mountain.

I sat down on the baron's ridiculous barrel throne and gazed around the room. "I am King Aethelfred," I said loudly.

I remembered the story about King Aethelfred and the insulting jester. The king had opened this very floor and dropped him out of sight to punish him for rudeness. That little ring in the floor must be part of King Aethelfred's trapdoor. But how could he open it while sitting on his throne? There must have been a button of some sort, probably something he could press with his foot.

I dropped to the floor and ran my fingers over the stones of the platform. One of them felt a tiny bit higher than the others. I pushed it with my thumb, but nothing happened. I stepped on it. Still nothing. Then I jumped on it.

With a loud snap, a square in front of the platform flopped downward. I ran to look and found a small stone room below the floor—a hole, really. Drifts of leaves filled the corners and dust and mouse droppings coated the floor.

Maybe I could hide in the little room. With a grin, I imagined smelly old Fulkes and the baron stomping around the castle searching for me, but I decided it wasn't a good idea. I wouldn't be able to close the trapdoor behind me, and I'd never get out again without a ladder or a rope.

I grabbed the ring and pulled the door shut. With another snap, it latched and looked just the same as before. It was a clever invention. I wished I could have seen the obnoxious jester's face when the floor fell out from underneath him.

Then I had a sudden brilliant idea. What if I dropped the baron down the hole? He'd be stuck and I could get away. I just had to think of a way to lure him over to the trapdoor while I pressed the button by the throne—too bad they were so far away from each other. I glanced wildly around the room. What would catch his attention enough to make him walk away from me?

My eye fell on the sword hanging on the wall behind the barrel. It looked like King Aethelfred's sword from the abbey. I remembered how Baron Thomas had held the sword so carefully and even talked to it. It was special to him.

I lifted the sword off the wall and wedged its point into a crack in the floor so the sword stood up, although it lurched sideways at a crazy angle. When the baron returned, he would have to cross the trapdoor to reach the sword. Then I could spring my trap.

There was only the smallest chance this plan would work, but I had to hope for the best. If I was going to die, I was going to die fighting—the only way I knew how.

Then the door to the throne room opened inward with a crash.

chapter twenty-three

Baron Thomas entered the room, his cloak rippling behind him like a giant red rose petal and his round face shining like a ripe apple. He plunked himself down on his barrel and sighed. "I wish your friend would hurry," he began, but stopped short. "What are you doing with that sword?" he hollered.

He strode over to the sword, yanked it out of the floor, and shook it at me. "This is King Aethelfred's sword! You dared to touch it!"

He was standing in the wrong place! I edged sideways, moving closer to the exit. The baron stepped toward me, still shaking the sword at me, too angry to speak. I took a step back. He took a step forward—then one more. He was finally in the right place, but now I was nowhere near the button.

I glanced over my shoulder to see if I should just run for the exit now, when the door crashed open again, letting a splash of afternoon sunshine into the dim room. A strange, shadowy figure loomed forward and the baron forgot about me as he squinted into the light.

It was now or never. I sprinted forward and took a flying leap, landing on the button. The trap door snapped open and the baron shot downward—but not far enough! His round body had gotten wedged inside the narrow opening. Now the baron's chest and shoulders stuck out of the ground like the stump of a tree.

"What is this?" he shouted, struggling to free himself. Then the strange figure stepped closer and we could see it clearly for the first time.

It was Kaye, dressed as a fool. But he wasn't wearing a hat with bells on it.

He wore a suit of armor, and over it, he wore something like a combination of a helmet and cloak. On his head perched a long-necked false donkey head, with a bristly mane, jutting yellow

teeth, and upright ears like a giant rabbit. An opening cut out of the front of the donkey's neck allowed Kaye to see and breathe.

Behind the donkey's head trailed a hairy-looking gray cape, that ended in stubby little stuffed legs with tiny hooves at the ends. The two front legs hung over Kaye's shoulders, and the two back legs and a stumpy tail hung down behind him, not quite touching the ground. He wore a bag with long straps slung across his chest. His sword hung at his hip.

Kaye had come for me! He was still my friend. And he had dressed like the worst kind of fool he could think of—Sir Donkey himself. He must have borrowed the costume from one of the Sir Donkeys at the masquerade last night.

When the baron realized the stranger was Kaye, he started giggling. He laughed until he turned purple, which looked terrible with his red cloak. The giant crown on his head slanted sideways as he laughed and slapped the stone floor in front of him. He couldn't stop. I realized that each time he shook with laughter, he slipped ever so slightly farther down the hole.

Kaye turned red with shame. But he stood straight and tall. "I'm glad you like my costume," he said. "Everyone I passed on the way here enjoyed it just as much as you do. I collected quite a crowd of admirers. They all cheered as I came up the mountain."

The baron laughed so hard he couldn't breathe anymore, but he managed to say between snorts, "Welcome, Sir Donkey. You look splendid. I was right—you are a far better fool than a knight. I hope you take my advice. Stop trying to be something you're not."

Kaye narrowed his eyes. "What about you?" he asked. "You think you're King Aethelfred. You dress like him and act like him and sit in his throne room, dreaming of the day you can rule his kingdom. Why can't you just be happy as a wool merchant back in Kingsbridge? That's who you really are."

"Silence, whelp!" the baron roared. "How dare you say such things? I am destined for greatness!"

"Well you don't look like it, stuck half in and half out of the ground like an onion," Kaye said. "You look as ridiculous as I do."

The baron growled with rage and began levering himself out of the hole. I ran up behind him and gave him a good push, hoping he'd fall all the way down the hole. He slid a little further, but he was just too big to fall down. He twisted around and grabbed my ankle so hard I thought my foot would break off.

"If I fall, you're going too!" he shouted.

I yanked my leg back, trying to twist away, but the baron held my ankle too tightly.

"Let him go if you want your edict!" Kaye said.

The baron let go of me so quickly, I fell over backward, banging my head against the stone floor. I sat up slowly, fighting a wave of dizziness. The room whirled around me as I watched Baron Thomas heave himself out of the trap by the elbows before bounding toward Kaye, bouncing like a turnip falling off a wagon. "I'll *have* that edict, and I'll kill you both!" he screamed as he whirled King Aethelfred's sword through the air and swung it violently at Kaye's head. The blow was true, and Kaye fell to the ground.

"NO!" I yelled, skittering on my hands and knees across the dusty floor to Kaye's side. The baron ignored me. He was busy sawing with his sword at the straps of the bag wrapped around Kaye's limp body. Once the baron cut the bag free, he crawled away and began digging through it like a badger.

I touched Kaye's shoulder. He didn't respond. I rocked him back and forth, trying to wake him. Nothing happened, so I summoned all my courage and looked at his wound. To my surprise, although the force of the blow had knocked him out, the rough hide of that ridiculous costume had turned the blade and saved Kaye's life.

I had to get Kaye out of there while the baron was busy with the bag. If Kaye hadn't brought the edicts, the baron would surely kill us. There would be no more laughing and joking and dressing in costumes. We had to run. I shook Kaye and slapped his face. Still nothing.

I noticed a chunk of the moldy cheese Fulkes had thrown at me lying on the floor. Maybe that would wake him. I grabbed the nubbin of cheese, crushed it between my fingers, and held the icky mess under Kaye's nose. After two breaths, he cracked his eyes open and made a face.

"What's going on? What's that smell?"

"Cheese!" I cried out, throwing my arms around him. "Can you walk? We have to go!"

But it was too late. The baron whirled around and roared at us. "Where is the edict?"

"Let us go and I'll give it to you," Kaye said.

"No," the baron said in return, a wily look in his eye. "Give it to me now or I'll crush your heads into jelly. Or better yet, I'll hurl you off the tower and let you crush your own heads when you land on them down in the king's garden among all the cabbages."

chapter twenty-four

Kaye stood up and walked with unsteady steps toward the door. I ran to support him. With a face as red as his cape, the baron screamed, "Don't walk away! You can't ignore me! I'm going to be king. PAY ATTENTION TO ME!"

Kaye shook his head at the baron. "You hate when people don't pay attention to you, don't you? That's the real reason you want to be king."

Baron Thomas grabbed Kaye's empty bag between his fists and tore it in half. "You're no different!" he screamed. "All *you* want is attention. That's why you're obsessed with being a knight. And when people laugh at you for being that idiotic Sir Donkey, you're still happy, because even that kind of attention is better than nothing!"

Kaye pinched his mouth shut and began walking toward the door again.

The baron leaped between us and the door, threatening us with his sword. "Admit it!" he challenged Kaye. "Say I'm right. I *know* I'm right. But I'll tell you something, my fine young fool—you're nothing but Sir Donkey and that's all you ever will be!"

Kaye shrugged. "I wasn't *supposed* to become Sir Donkey. I wanted to be a knight like my father."

"You'll never be anything like your father," the baron hissed, shifting closer to us. "You're a joke and a laughingstock. Look at you, running away from a fight. Your father would never flee!

He would stand and fight—like a man and a knight! You must be such a disappointment to him. You'll never be *anything* like him."

Kaye flinched but raised his head and met the baron's eyes. "No," he said slowly. "My father wouldn't run away. But I'm not strong enough to fight you. This is the only way I can help my friend. I may never be like my father, no matter how hard I try, but there are thousands of ways to be a good knight. I can find my own way. I don't have to copy anyone."

The baron and I both stared at Kaye in surprise. "What are you talking about?" the baron huffed, pointing to the donkey costume on Kaye's head. "You're only Sir Donkey. You'll always be Sir Donkey. You'll never be any good as a *real* knight."

Kaye nodded. "Perhaps. But that is what I am. I don't have to copy anyone else. And neither do you. You don't have to wear that ridiculous false crown. You don't have to wear Aethelfred's robe and sit on Aethelfred's throne and wave Aethelfred's sword around."

"Yes, I do," the baron scowled. "I'm his heir. Give me the edict, and I'll prove it. The monks found it on the Bishop of Newksbury when they fished him out of the well. They searched for me for many years before they found me. The abbot said it was the will of heaven for me to be found just as I was about to have enough money to raise an army to take my throne and become king." Then the baron frowned, "But you took that money when you stole those rubies. I should kill you now."

"No," Kaye said. "There's something you need to know. You keep talking about the edict, but we took two edicts from the abbey, both signed by the Bishop of Newksbury."

"What are you talking about?" the baron asked, looking genuinely confused.

Kaye reached into his shirt and pulled out the two edicts. "They're here. One says that the kingdom will remain divided and the king hopes the bishop's edict will help the people accept that. The other says that the king regrets his decision and instead reunites the kingdom and leaves the throne to his youngest son Enulf."

"Why are there two?" the baron asked.

"I don't know," Kaye said, holding one of them in the air, "but this one about Enulf doesn't look like it ever fell down a well. It looks new and fresh, whereas this one that confirms the divided kingdom," he said, holding up the other parchment, "looks like it's been drowned and carefully blotted dry."

"Let me see!" the baron cried out, rushing over to Kaye. He leaned over Kaye's shoulder and groaned. "That can't be! I don't understand." His anguish turned to rage as he chewed on his lip before yelling out, "Blast that lying abbot! I hope he's eaten alive by worms!"

Kaye quietly folded up the parchments and slid them inside his shirt, under his armor. Together we edged away from the baron and toward the door.

"Stop!" the baron yelled, leaping towards us. "Give me those parchments. I will still be king. It is my right! I am King Aethelfred's descendant and I will reunite the kingdom. It is the duty given me by heaven!"

"But you're not the heir," Kaye said.

"Don't bandy words with me, whelp!" the baron said, hitting Kaye on the side of the head with his fist. "Give me the edicts. I saw you hide them. I'll destroy the old edict. All I need is the new one to prove I'm the heir. No one will ever know!"

"We'll know!" I cried out.

He made a face at me. "Then you know too much," the baron replied. "I'll feed your livers to the sparrows before I let you leave here alive."

The room dimmed as a figure filled the door. "I don't think so," a deep voice said. It was Sir Henry, come to save us! He strode into the room. The baron edged behind me.

I looked at Kaye, thinking he'd be so pleased that his father was there to save the day, but he just looked sad. "At least you'll be safe, Reggie," he said. "I'm sorry I couldn't rescue you."

"What does it matter?" I whispered.

"It doesn't, as long as you're safe," he said with a little laugh. "I don't think I'll ever have a chance to show my father anything good about myself. I always look the fool in front of him. Maybe that's my own special skill as a knight."

I realized that once again, Kaye was humiliated in front of his father—a weak, young child, dressed in a ridiculous costume, just like a little boy playing at being a knight.

I pulled at the knots holding the donkey costume around Kaye's neck. "At least take that thing off," I said. The knots finally gave way and the horrible thing fell in a hairy heap on the floor.

"Ah, Sir Henry," the baron said, his voice purring like a large, brilliantly red cat. "You've come to save your son, I see. Well, you'll soon have him. I'm no match for you with a sword. We all know that." He sighed and gazed at King Aethelfred's sword that he still held in his hand. "What a pity—to have such a fine sword and to lack the skill to use it." He gave Kaye a look and Kaye blushed as red as the baron's normal face.

"Drop the sword, Thomas," Sir Henry said, his voice as stern as stone. "I've come to arrest you for attempting to murder King Aldric."

"I'm dropping it, I'm dropping it," the baron said, flinging the sword away. It skidded across the floor and fell into the open trapdoor. While we stared at it, the baron snatched a knife out of his boot, grabbed me from behind and pressed the cold blade to my throat. It hurt. Not only was it sharp, but he held it so tightly against my neck that I could barely breathe. "This is your fault," the baron hissed, his breath hot against my face. "You stopped the joust, you wrote that letter—you said no one could read it but the donkey knight. It's your fault the real knight showed up. You deceived me!"

"So…did…the…abbot…" I managed to say.

The baron grabbed my hair, yanked my head back and pressed the blade even harder against my neck. "Get out of my way," he said. "Let me go or I'll kill him."

chapter twenty-five

Kaye and Sir Henry stepped aside and the baron dragged me out into the watery sunlight of the courtyard. The crumbling gates on the far side of the courtyard led to the road that went down the mountain to the new castle.

On the other side of the broken wall, I heard voices like the sound of a crowd at a party. I heard faint strains of music and laughter. I had forgotten that King Aldric opened part of the old castle for visitors because of King Aethelfred's Day of Remembrance. I smelled fried dough on a small breeze and despite all the danger I was in, my mouth watered. I tried to swallow, but it hurt.

Here in the courtyard, all was silent as the baron dragged me toward the gate. Sir Henry followed closely, but not close enough to make the baron decide to kill me. Kaye walked next to him, a living shadow. Once the baron neared the gate, he said to Kaye, "Give me those edicts. I know you have them. I saw you put them in your armor."

Sir Henry looked around and realized Kaye was there too. "Get behind me, Kaye," he said sharply. "I'll take care of this."

The baron laughed. "No, you won't! If you try taking care of anything, I'll kill this boy. You can't allow that, can you? Surely you don't want to arrest me so badly that you'd let a child die. I know you. You're the perfect knight. And your son there—he copies you in every possible way, so he'll never do anything to make me kill this boy either. So I'm safe from anything either of you can do. Give me the edicts and I'll go."

"Don't do anything, Kaye," Sir Henry barked.

"It's not true," Kaye said.

"What's not true?" both Sir Henry and the baron asked at the same time.

"I *have* always tried to copy my father. He's a perfect knight, and I've wanted so badly to be just like him. But now I'm Sir Donkey, and my father may never be proud of me for being just like him."

"Oh, Kaye," Sir Henry said softly.

The baron laughed. "We all know you're useless as a knight, boy, so stop crying about it."

I squinted over the baron's arm at Kaye. "He's not crying," I grunted at the baron.

"Hold your tongue," the baron growled in my ear.

"No," Kaye said. "I'm not useless. I can be a good knight in my own way. I have my own strengths. And that means I can do something my father would never do." He laid his sword down on the ground and walked toward the baron with his hands held out.

"What are you doing, Kaye?" Sir Henry said.

"Stay back!" the baron warned Sir Henry, pressing the flat of the knife even harder against my throat. I gagged.

Sir Henry froze. Kaye kept approaching. When he stood just in front of us, he said to the baron, "Take me."

"What?" the baron said incredulously.

"Take me," Kaye repeated. "The edicts are inside my armor. You want a hostage. You want the edicts. Take me instead of Reggie. Then you'll have both the things you want."

I could feel the baron thinking as his hot breath huffed and puffed against my ear. "Step aside," he said to Kaye, removing the knife from my throat and setting his foot on my backside. With a tremendous push, he shoved me away from him and grabbed Kaye, setting the knife against *his* throat. I hit the ground with a thud, banging my chin and biting my tongue. I tasted blood, but whipped around to see what would happen to Kaye.

"I have what I want," the baron said. "I'm leaving now. If you come anywhere near me, the boy dies. Do you understand?"

Sir Henry and I nodded, but as soon as the baron was outside the gates, we followed him. I hoped Kaye had a great plan up his sleeve along with those edicts, but he didn't do anything until they reached the middle of the largest crowd on the path.

Then Kaye shouted, "Save me, people of Eldridge. This man tried to murder your king!"

The crowd gasped in horror as they realized what was happening right in their midst.

"He has a knife!" someone called out.

A woman screamed. "What's he doing with that boy?"

"Stop him!" a third voice cried out. A stone flew through the air and hit the baron on the shoulder.

I barely realized that Beau had thrown it when I saw two familiar faces. It was Walter and his mum from the forest, who had once stopped our saddlebag thief. They hurled stones at the baron for all they were worth. "Leave that boy alone!" they cried out. "He's our friend."

The rest of the crowd joined in, shouting at the baron in anger, "You tried to kill our king!" and, "*You're* the pretender!" and, "We want our money!" Those voices must have belonged to men from the baron's unpaid army.

Then a particularly large stone sailed through the air and hit the baron on the side of his head. The enormous crown took most of the blow, but it was enough to knock him off balance.

The baron dropped Kaye and fell to the road, and the crowd set upon him, kicking him and hitting him with their walking sticks.

Sir Henry rushed forward to rescue the baron, waving the crowds back and tying the baron's hands firmly behind him. "Leave him, good people," Sir Henry said. "Let the king choose his own justice for this would-be murderer." The crowd murmured their agreement and drew back to give Sir Henry space.

He told two stout men to keep an eye on the baron, who sat in the middle of the road looking forlorn, his crown dented and off-center, the blood-bright stones in it cracked and shattered. They were only glass after all.

Then Sir Henry knelt in the road beside Kaye. I pushed through the crowd until I was next to them. A trickle of red blood ran down Kaye's forehead and dripped off the end of his nose. Sir Henry pulled a soft cloth from his sleeve and pressed it to Kaye's forehead. "Are you all right?" he asked.

Kaye nodded. "It was just a stray stone," he said. He ran a fingertip over his forehead. "Now I'll have matching scars up here," he said with a sad laugh. "Two scars for being a bad knight. One for being bad at my knight training, and one for being Sir Donkey."

"Kaye," Sir Henry said, "that was a brave and noble thing you did. You saved Reggie's life when I couldn't. I would never have thought of doing that. You're a fine knight and a fine friend. I couldn't ask for anything more than that. I'm so proud of you."

Kaye smiled up at his father from under the cloth on his forehead and then threw his arms around him. "I'm sorry," he whispered. "I tried so hard to be like you. I just can't do it."

Sir Henry folded Kaye close in his arms. "You should be your own kind of knight," he said. "You know that now. I'm sorry if

I ever made you think differently. I never meant to train you to be just like me. I was training you to become a *better* knight than me—a knight who doesn't have to fight all the time. But then I got so caught up in trying to make a peaceful world where you could actually be that kind of knight that I hurt you more than I helped you. I'm so sorry. I should have been there for you."

Kaye buried his face in Sir Henry's shoulder, leaving a streak of blood on his father's cheek. Sir Henry rested his face on Kaye's gingery head and whispered, "I'm so glad you're safe."

chapter twenty-six

Sir Henry stood up and helped Kaye to his feet. In a loud voice he said, "Come now, let us all escort this man to meet the king's justice."

The crowd cheered and followed Sir Henry and Kaye down the mountain road. I was about to join them when someone almost pushed me sideways off my feet. "Hey!" I said, my voice creaking like a broken bellows.

"What happened to your voice?" Beau asked.

"It's my throat," I croaked. "I had a knife smashed up against it. It hurts, you know."

Beau smiled and shrugged. "Oh, no, I wouldn't know. I've never tried it myself."

"Where have you been?" I asked.

"You mean while you were almost getting yourselves killed?" he asked with a raised eyebrow. "Let's see—first I found your note that Kaye dropped when he left the ambassador's meeting and went after you without a word to anyone. Then I spent a while trying to read your handwriting."

"You could read it?" I asked in wonder.

"No," Beau said. "But I knew it was possible, because Kaye can read it, so I kept trying. Eventually I found the words 'Baron Thomas' and 'old castle' and then I ran to Sir Henry and he charged up the mountain after you like a dragon. I followed him. I hope you saw me throw the first stone at that fool of a baron."

"I did," I said. "Good job, Beau."

Most of the crowd had gone down the mountain, but as we prepared to follow them, I laid a hand on Beau's arm. "Wait," I said. "Kaye just saved my life. I want to do something for him, but I need your help. And your cloak."

Beau unpinned his cloak and held it out to me. "What do you want to do?" he asked.

"I want to kill Sir Donkey," I told him, and grinned as his mouth fell open.

"You want to kill Kaye?" he asked.

I shook my head. "No, I want to kill Sir Donkey. Everyone in the crowd saw Sir Donkey walk up the mountain, but even though people know Kaye and Sir Donkey are the same person, if they see Sir Donkey being carried down the mountain and think that he died, maybe Kaye can have a fresh start as Sir Kaye."

Beau laughed. "What a wonderful idea. So how do we kill Sir Donkey?"

"Come with me," I said, leading the way back to the old throne room, where Kaye's Sir Donkey costume lay in a pile on the floor. "There's our body," I said, pointing to it. "We just need to make it look like it was a person while we carry it down the mountain."

"We need a bier," Beau said.

"What's that?"

"We'll get two long sticks and tie cloth flat between them to make a kind of bed we can carry the body on," Beau explained. "One of us can carry the front end of the sticks and one of us can carry the back end."

"That's perfect!" I said. We found two visitors in the public part of the old castle who had walked up the mountain leaning on long walking sticks. They didn't want to lose them, but when we explained we needed the sticks to make a bier, they felt bad and let us have them.

Beau and I tied my cloak between the sticks and laid the donkey costume on top of it. I covered it with Beau's cloak. "It's too flat," Beau said. "No one will think there's a body under there. We need to stuff it with something."

I looked around. "There's not much up here but leaves and rocks," I said. "The leaves will be too flat…" I trailed off as we looked at each other.

And that's how we ended up carrying a bier full of rocks down the mountain. Part of the head, ears, and one leg of the donkey costume stuck out from the cloak we spread over the rocks—just enough for anyone watching to know that we did indeed carry Sir Donkey down the mountain to the king's castle.

By the time we reached the bottom of the mountain and the entrance to the new castle, my arms felt like they had stretched out until my hands hung down to my knees, but I didn't say anything. I just let the burning feeling of blisters growing on my fingers make my face look as sad as possible, which was proper, considering that someone had died.

Festival-going crowds flocked through the gates in the outer wall, heading to the jousts and other displays of knightly skills on the lists. "Make way," Beau called out loudly, in a deep voice. "Make way for the body of Sir Donkey, who died at the hands of Baron Thomas while defending the king's honor. Make way for Sir Donkey, the dead knight."

I let my face stretch out as long as my arms were feeling while we made our way slowly through the crowd that wept in sympathy for the mysterious fallen hero. The name Baron Thomas

swept through the whispering throngs and was accompanied by a great deal of hissing. I was willing to guess that there was no one more unpopular in Eldridge right now than Baron Thomas.

Eventually we reached the main castle gates, but rumors of our approach had arrived before us. The guards let us through, and the king's steward himself came to greet us. "Come, put Sir Donkey in a room by himself where he can lie in state," he told us in low, solemn tones.

I had to fight back a laugh, but I couldn't ruin this. Sir Donkey may not have been real, but it was important for him to be dead.

We followed the steward across the great hall with our heavy burden. He left us in a small room off the corridor where I had gotten lost the night I was kidnapped. We were just about to set the bier down on a table when Kaye burst into the room. He wore a bandage around his head.

"Where have you been?" he asked. "I've been waiting for you for hours. They wouldn't let me leave to find you because of my head. They said I should rest it and not be riding or walking much for a few days, and I just saw you crossing the great hall and—what is *that?*" He finally noticed what we carried between us.

Beau shook his head sadly. "Our dear, dead friend, Sir Donkey," he said.

"He died at the hands of Baron Thomas while defending the king's honor. It was a noble death, but alas, we shall hear no more of Sir Donkey's great deeds," I said.

Kaye stared at our burden and then looked up at us, his eyes alight with happiness. "Who did this?" he whispered.

"We did," I said.

"Reggie," Beau said at the same time.

"We did it for you," I said.

Beau and I hefted the bier onto the table and I began rubbing my arms to get the feeling back into them. Kaye lifted a corner of Beau's cloak and peeked underneath. "You've been carrying a pile of rocks under here?" he said in amazement.

"Rocks *and* blocks," I said. "From the old castle walls."

Kaye grinned. "Well, Sir Donkey always was a bit of a block-head, wasn't he?" Then he laughed, sounding happier than he had in weeks. "Poor Sir Donkey," he said. "We'll have to make sure he gets a decent burial."

"I think King Aldric might be very happy to help with that," Beau said with a smile.

chapter twenty-seven

The king thought burying Sir Donkey was a huge joke and he was more than happy to help plan a funeral suitable for a hero. Many people showed up to see Sir Donkey buried outside the castle chapel. The king spoke a few words, thanking Sir Donkey for his sacrifice, and the body—now hidden inside a wooden coffin—was placed in the ground.

Two dukes, an earl, several knights of Eldridge, and Sir Henry carried the coffin from the chapel to the gravesite. After they set the coffin down, I heard the earl complain to one of the dukes about how heavy the coffin was. I covered my mouth with my hand so no one would see me smile.

After that, we stayed with King Aldric for a while, and Kaye rested his head, as the surgeons had recommended. The king's guards soon tracked down Fulkes and Birket and our horses, which we were very glad to get back.

At Kaye's request, King Aldric sent some trusted guards back to Kingsbridge to open up the baron's warehouse using the key Azam had given Kaye.

The warehouse was mostly filled with wool, as Azam had said, and the guards left that alone until the king could decide what to do with it, but the guards also found King Aethelfred's throne, as well as a locked chest containing some other items that had belonged to the dead king. They brought the throne and the chest back to Rombauer Castle.

We gathered around the king as he opened up the chest on the day it arrived. At first glance, it was disappointing.

"It's just old armor," Kaye said.

The king lifted piece after piece of armor out of the chest. "Yes, but it's all here. We could put it together and let the people of Eldridge see it on the next Day of Remembrance. Aethelfred is still a greatly beloved king here in Eldridge, despite the fact that he divided the kingdom. I don't believe anyone alive now is sorry that he did that, except for that wretched Baron Thomas."

"What will you do with Baron Thomas, Your Majesty?" Sir Henry asked the king.

"I will decide that in good time," the king replied. "For now, he is safely locked in the tower, and I will take care of him when I am ready. Do not fear. Justice will be swift. I will not forget that he tried to kill me and then blame you, my good friend."

"Look!" I said, pouncing on something bright in the corner of the box. It was a small circle of gold set with three tiny balas rubies. "It's Aethelfred's crown!" I started laughing. "No wonder Baron Thomas made a different crown for himself. This one wasn't nearly big enough or important enough for him to wear!"

"Baron Thomas could have worn this crown as a bracelet!" Beau said with a laugh as he slid it onto his arm.

"Here's a shield at the bottom," Kaye said, lifting it out.

"Ah, see how small it is? That is an old shield indeed," the king breathed, reaching for it. He ran his fingers over the undecorated front of the shield. "Look how battered the metal is," he said. "And such a plain shield for a king to carry! Truly he must have been a humble king, a hard-working king. No wonder the people loved him."

King Aldric slid his arm through the shield's straps, grasped the handle, and held it in front of him. "Not a single jewel or carving on it," he marveled again. "No, wait, there is something written inside the shield." He squinted at the old writing and read aloud. "It says that only the best and most worthy of knights may carry this shield."

The king looked up at Sir Henry and smiled. "Perhaps you should have this," he said. "You have always proven yourself to be the best and most worthy of knights and the best and most worthy of friends."

Sir Henry smiled and bowed. "I thank you, my friend, Your Majesty," he said, reaching for the shield, "but I would like to give this to Sir Kaye. He has proven himself over and over again to be one of the best and most worthy of knights in a way that is his very own. I think we should honor him for that."

The king nodded, and Sir Henry knelt and presented the shield to Kaye. "Bear it well, my son," he said.

Kaye took the shield carefully in both hands and tried it out, holding it in front of him, his face shining with happiness.

"It's the perfect size for you," the king remarked, his beady eyes alive with interest, like a bird that has just spotted something shiny it can carry away to its nest.

Then the king said to Sir Henry, "My friend, I would like to give you a gift as well. Your services have been of great help to the country of Eldridge. Tell me, is there anything at all that I can do for you?"

Sir Henry glanced at Kaye, who defended himself with his shield while Beau pretended to strike him with a sword. "Yes, Your Majesty, I have a request," he said.

"What is it?" the king asked.

"I would like to return to my family. Here my son has grown to become a knight without me, and I have a wife and daughter at home. I miss them. They need me. I need them."

Kaye fell silent as he stared intently at the king and waited for his reply.

"This is a surprise, Sir Henry," the king said. "Your former king, Frederick, and your new queen Vianne both assured me that you were committed to helping me keep the peace between our kingdoms and others. You have done well all this time. We would not have had a peace this long or this strong without your help and counsel. I fear I must not let you go."

Kaye's face fell, and Sir Henry bowed quietly, looking at the floor. He glanced up sharply at the king's next words. "However, I cannot keep a man from his family. You may return to your home."

"Oh, Father!" Kaye shouted, running to his side. "You're coming home!"

The king climbed stiffly to his feet. "I still need your help, Sir Henry," he cautioned him. "You must come back here at least four months out of the year." He held up a finger. "But when you return, you must come with your family. Will that do?"

Sir Henry reached over Kaye's head to grasp the king's hands. "Thank you, Your Majesty. Thank you, my friend. Thank you for my family."

Beau and I cheered together, "Hooray! Sir Henry finally returns to Knox! And Sir Kaye, the best and most worthy of knights!"

Kaye and Sir Henry both laughed out loud, one laugh deep, the other somewhere in the middle. They didn't sound at all alike, but together they sounded just right.

the end

aBout tHe autHor

Don M. Winn is the award-winning author of twelve children's picture books, including *Superhero*; *The Higgledy-Piggledy Pigeon*; *Twitch the Squirrel and the Forbidden Bridge*; *Space Cop Zack, Protector of the Galaxy*; and *GARG's Secret Mission*.

The Eldridge Conspiracy is his fourth novel for middle readers in the *Sir Kaye the Boy Knight* series. *The Knighting of Sir Kaye*, *The Lost Castle Treasure*, and *Legend of the Forest Beast* are the first three books in the series.

Don currently lives with his family in Round Rock, Texas.

Visit his website at **www.donwinn.com** for more information and all the latest news. If you liked this book, he'd love to hear from you.

You can e-mail him at **author@donwinn.com**.

Don't miss Sir Kaye the Boy Knight® Book One:
The Knighting of Sir Kaye

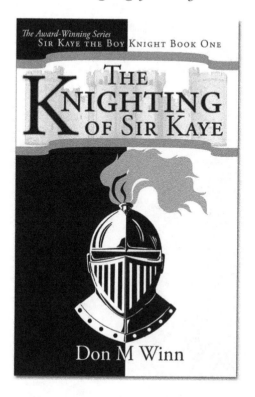

When the new queen of Knox knights 12-year-old Kaye for doing a brave deed, he may be in over his head. Can he hold his own against all the other knights who hate him? Can he outwit the terrible Sir Melchor and defeat him in the tournament?

An IndieReader Discovery Award Winner
A Moonbeam Children's Book Award Winner
A UK Wishing Shelf Award Winner

"Fortitude, good will, and friendship triumph in this enjoyable story."
— *Publishers Weekly*

"A lively and adventurous kids' book, full of gentle humor and warmth."
— *IndieReader Review*

"A fantastic, fun-filled adventure. Highly recommended."
— *The Wishing Shelf Book Award*

Don't miss Sir Kaye the Boy Knight® Book Two:
The Lost Castle Treasure

The treasure house of Knox castle is empty! As Kaye searches for the missing treasure, jealous knights plot to get rid of him for good. Can Kaye find the treasure in time to save the kingdom? Or will he lose his knighthood forever?

A Foreword Reviews Indiefab Book of the Year Finalist
A UK Wishing Shelf Award Finalist • A Readers' Favorite Finalist

"A fun, exciting adventure. Sir Kaye is a fantastic role model for kids."
—*The Wishing Shelf Book Award*

"Has all the ingredients to make it an exciting read for children: mystery, adventure, intrigue, suspense and three interesting characters."
—*Readers' Favorite Review*

Don't miss Sir Kaye the Boy Knight® Book Three:
Legend of the Forest Beast

Kaye's tutor is missing! Kaye, Reggie, and Beau set out to find him. Puzzling prisoners, rumors of a mysterious beast, and one very determined girl make this the adventure of a lifetime.

A Moonbeam Children's Book Award Winner
A Mom's Choice Gold Medal Award Winner

"A cracking, fun-filled adventure. Highly recommended!"

—*The Wishing Shelf Book Award*

"*Legend of the Forest Beast* captures colorful adventures, fun characters, and inspirational thoughts in a quick and easy read for children."

—*IndieReader Review*

CPSIA information can be obtained
at www.ICGtesting.com
Printed in the USA
LVHW010809180820
663479LV00006B/386